Cuffed
Book One

By: Carissa McIntyre

Thank you to everyone who saw me through this journey; I would never have come this far without you. Much love.

Cover Model: Jess Lynne
Photographer: Nathan Mann Mannnatjphoto

Copyright March 2017 Carissa McIntyre
Fourth Edition Published August 2020
Self Published by Lady Mack Xo
All Rights Reserved, including the right of reproduction in whole or in part in any form.
Wrote in Canada
Manufactured in the USA
All Rights Reserved

Carissa McIntyre is a self-published author from Ontario Canada. Her work can be found at
www.ladymackxo.com
Publishing / all other inquiries may be sent to:
ladymackxo@gmail.com

New Adult – Romance -Erotica

Copyright 2017 by Carissa McIntyre
All Rights Reserved

ISBN-13: 978-1544621401
ISBN-10: 154462140X

Cuffed
Book One

Chapter One:
Saturday, Before Midnight

Demi's struggling; she's tugging and pulling her arms, feeling the cuffs bite into the skin around her wrists, trying to break free. She moans loudly, attempting to fight, but she cannot escape her restraints. She's blindfolded, and her cold body shivers in the darkness. There is nothing but silence all around her. Handcuffs are tugging roughly against her ankles too, keeping her totally pinned to the bed, spread eagle style. She finds herself helpless. The sheets are damp with sweat and twisted all around her. Her skin is cool and covered in goosebumps, yet she feels warm from her need and her lust, the sexual tension that's consuming her, and the blood pumping fast through her veins. Her nipples are rock hard, begging to be pinched, or to be bit, or just to be touched. She twists against her restraints again, desperate, making little whimpers and crying out for someone. Aching for release.

She thinks she hears something. There's a few soft noises coming from beside her. She sucks her breath in hard, holds it, keeping herself still in anticipation. Then there's pressure beside her as some stranger climbs onto the bed. His warm breath seems to be all over her, teasing her sweaty skin, but he never quite comes close enough to touch her. No lips, no tongue, only his breath. He just keeps teasing her, always out of her reach. She pulls at her restraints wildly, whimpering, trying to force her hips upwards to connect with him. She longs for him, his touch, his tongue, his fingers, she needs to feel him, all of him, to have him inside of her, to be filled by his cock, to cum. But she is left hanging, her body aching, her pussy wet, desperately wanting more, but getting nothing.

¤¤¤

Demi wakes in a startled huff, covered in sweat and goosebumps and tangled within the sheets that are wrapped tightly around her, just like they had been in her dream. Her breathing is heavy, gasping almost, and her body aches with longing for that sexual release that never came. Her pussy is damp and throbbing between her legs. She throws herself back on the bed and lashes out at the sheets, kicking off her pajama pants as well, leaving herself stripped to just her nightgown and underwear. Frustration and anger mix with the sexual aching that's flourishing through her veins.

The room is dark, and as there's no one else here with her, the entire house lies in silence. Even at 26, she's still living in her childhood home and her mother has gone away on vacation, although she is due to fly back in the morning. Her mother has been traveling almost nonstop since her father passed away just over a year ago, and Demi finds herself here alone more often than not, with no close friends or serious boyfriends in her life either. The quiet doesn't normally get to her, but tonight it does. She is tired of being alone.

Demi forces herself to take some long deep slow breaths to calm her heart beat and her emotions. All of this raw energy that keeps her awake and restless at night comes from her choice of past relationships and partners and her inability to break the patterns she is in. And a lot of *that* stems from unresolved issues from her family, and her dad's death. She can thank a year of therapy since his passing for teaching her more about her failed relationships than anything else.

When it comes to sex, for her the bottom line always seems to be that as soon as the cuffs come out of her drawer, or she brings up the idea of bondage, or BDSM, or anything too out of the ordinary or maybe too taboo for the vanilla minded, the guys go running. She gets labeled as a freak, like some kind of slut. She always seems to attract the most "dominant bad boys" on the outside, but once they get alone with her behind closed doors they are as vanilla as ice cream, and just as soft. That macho attitude always seems to come from their own issues, and not any actual desire to be sexually dominant to a submissive. Demi's been so unsatisfied with her sex life her whole life, but she just doesn't seem to know how to break free from those routines she's been following, and she hasn't got that far with her therapist yet.

She tells herself to let the dream go and tries to get comfortable, but she only ends up rolling over and over and over in her bed, unable to shake it off or to break herself free of the emotions that she's feeling. She isn't sure if she should masturbate to dull the ache between her legs, or if it will make it worse; masturbating doesn't seem to satisfy her anymore, but she doesn't know if she can fall asleep like this either.

She glances over at the clock on her nightstand and sees that it reads 11:45pm. How is it not even midnight yet? She thinks to herself. She hadn't even been sleeping for very long before she was woken up by that crazy dream. She has to get back to bed and get some actual sleep, since she has to be up at 6am in order to get to the airport for her mother's flight back home at 7am. Demi moans aloud and rolls back over again. And then again. And then again. She knows that even if she brings out some toys and plays with herself for hours, she still won't be as satisfied as a really good tie me up, take me and fuck me senseless session would leave her. And that's exactly what she's craving deep down inside.

And yet, only a few moments later, she finds herself reaching down her stomach to satisfy that ache that's calling out from between her thighs. She's never been very good at taking directions from herself anyway, and that's where her submissive side comes out in the bedroom.

She finds her soft lips swollen and moist, and she spreads them and moans as her fingers move back and forth from her clit to her wet hole, slowly teasing and bringing herself closer and closer to release. She imagines that scene she was dreaming about earlier, only this time the stranger makes contact with her, taking her, pounding into her, using her, forcing her to cum over and over again. In reality she cums hard around her fingers, grabbing out at the bedding around her and thrusting her body out against nothing but air.

When she's done, she still finds herself feeling as sexually frustrated and miserable as she was before. She cleans herself up, falling into a bit of a depressed and grumpy funk thinking about her current life. Climbing back into bed, she tosses and turns for a while and eventually falls back into a restless, but thankfully, dreamless sleep.

Chapter Two:
Sunday, just after midnight

Demi feels strong hands take hold of her, slowly rousing her from her slumber as she is taken roughly from her bed. She's grabbed around the arms by someone, and then something covers her face; soft and very dark, it seems like a hood of sorts. It pulls tight around her throat, but not tight enough to choke her, just tight enough to keep it in place. Then a hand presses up against her mouth, pushing the fabric into her lips, constricting her breathing and stopping her from making a sound as she slowly comes to her senses. She feels her arms pulled together tightly in front of her, and then cuffed, and that starts to bring her out of her sleepy fog.

For a split second she wonders if she may still be dreaming again, another teasing encounter to leave her feeling empty and miserable; maybe this time it will be a not really forced gang bang or a couple of lesbians taking her in the dressing room, or something else just as kinky and different than her normal boring routine. But then a smell hits her nose, something unexpected and *real;* it's the smell of cheap cologne. There is a discomfort as she's lifted and picked up into someone's arms, and that finally snaps her fully awake. She's being grabbed by strangers, she's being taken from her own bedroom, this is real!

Demi becomes disoriented as she's carried like a child, with a hand still covering her mouth, and her bare legs left cold and dangling in the air. Demi's eyes snap open and nothing but complete darkness surrounds her; she really is bound and captive, and this is not another sexy dream or a fantasy. She's no longer horny, she's scared, and she doesn't understand why this is happening to her.

Despite the cuffs and the hands that are holding her tightly and everything else working against her, she still struggles and fights; pushing against her captor, kicking her legs out trying to connect with something, and attempting to scream, whatever she thinks may help her get out of this situation. Her taker just pins her tighter against him. He seems to be built well and clearly has no issues carrying her and throwing her around like a rag doll.

Demi feels everything shift as they move out of her bedroom. The world begins to bounce as they start to descend down the stairs to the front door. No!!! She's screaming inside her head, she can't let them take her, what the hell are they going to do to her? And she's in her damn nightgown! She feels so exposed, and terrified. She struggles with all of her might, trying to kick and fight, but all her attempts to escape are useless.

She hears footsteps of the guy carrying her first, and then there's a second set behind him as they cross the tiled entrance way. Then the cool night air hits her bare skin as they leave the house, and she starts to panic again. She hears the door being pulled shut behind them, and then that bounce again as they rush quietly down the back driveway, the one that's hidden from sight of any neighbors from the shelter of the house and bushes.

She wonders where they are going. She listens closely but still only hears two sets of footsteps. They stop for a moment and there is a shuffle, then she hears the sound of a sliding door and she's placed on the cold hard metal in the back of a vehicle. She feels the shift as someone gets in beside her. Again, she thinks of escaping; running blindfolded even, or just screaming for someone to help her, and she takes a deep breath to do just that as soon as her mouth is uncovered, but they had thought of that. "You are going to be quiet and sit still," a gruff voice says from beside her. It seems like a good time to do as she is told as she feels something press up against her side, cold, circular... a gun. That's all the encouragement she needs, and she swallows the urge to scream.

She feels the rumble of the vehicle beneath her as it starts up and then they are off, pulling out of her driveway and turning left. She shivers, filled with terror and feelings of uncertainty and the disorientation of moving around while blindfolded. Demi tries to pay attention to where they are going, but once they turn a few times and have been traveling for a while she is lost in the sway as they leave the safety of her house and her life, driving through the night with two strangers, headed to who knows where.

Adam sits beside her in the back of the van, curled up against the side, his gun drawn and pointed at her, but he doesn't make a sound. He feels like he's on guard duty. He watches her shake and shiver, her legs breaking out in goosebumps, pale sexy legs covered in goosebumps that seem to go up and up forever before they end at what looks like a pair of pink frilly panties. Shit, he thinks to himself, the goosebumps breaking his train of thought, she isn't even wearing anything more than a nightie? What the hell. They should have thought to bring or grab her clothes if they were going to be snatching her out of her bed at night like this.

His cock grows hard despite feeling bad for her; she is thin, pretty, and helpless, and half naked... Bound and pinned... And it has been a long time since he has really had a good rump in the hay. Hell, it's been a long time since he's had a lousy one at that. How is he not supposed to react to the scene right here in front of him?

He feels guilty at the thought, but he's grateful that no one can see him blush. Before this even started, he and his partner had to have a long embarrassing chat about how Adam needs to keep his dick and his emotions in check. It hasn't even been a whole ten minutes yet, and now here he is, already sexualizing things. Does he really need to start repeating to himself all the scolding's he's already received from his buddy? Because he knows Brandon would have no problem scolding him right now if he found out.

She shakes against the side of the van, and watching her shiver is breaking through his horny fog and self-pity party and tugging at the strings in his heart. He hates that he can be so soft inside, and so not in control of his emotions. He grabs one of the blankets that Brandon has stashed in the back of the van and throws it over her legs. He can't watch her suffer in this cold, even if he is enjoying the view, and even if they are kidnapping her. They aren't planning on harming her and they aren't monsters, this was all just supposed to be an exchange for money, and it's going to take more than a few minutes to drive out to the house they plan to hold up at. She will be frozen by then if he doesn't cover her up.

He sees her jump from the shock of the blanket touching her, then she seems to withdraw even more against the back of the van, tied up and huddled up. Silent and scared. He watches her the entire trip, never taking his eyes off of her, keeping his gun pointed at her, swaying and leaning into the turns and bumps, and never saying a word to her. He makes sure to keep his distance so that they don't touch. He wonders what she could possibly been thinking about. Then he wonders why he even cares.

Suddenly something sort of dawns on him; if he was a woman, he'd probably be thinking that they were going to rape him or something... isn't that what's all over the news these days? Isn't that what's bred into women's minds? He has a younger sister, and he's heard his fair share of horror stories growing up, and even now about the dating world. He urgently feels they need to tell her that this is only a kidnapping, and that they aren't going to hurt her, hell they should have right when they woke her, why hadn't they thought of that? Adam finds himself feeling even more guilty, and a bit ashamed, and then scolds himself for acting so stupid. He isn't in charge here, not really, and he can't think of everything.

The van may be silent, but Demi's head is anything but. As she lies against the side of the moving vehicle, curled up into a ball underneath the blanket for warmth, hands balled into fists, she finds she's filled with such conflicting thoughts. Part of her is wondering exactly the same thing Adam is imagining she is; did they plan to rape her? But then again, if that's all they are after, why not just do it at her house, in her bed? The house was empty, and no one was around. Why go to all this trouble to take her in the dead of the night, tie her up, and drive off somewhere with her? Where were they even taking her, that she needs to be blindfolded for? She has no idea what's going on, but she knows that there has to be something far more to this than what she's imagining.

Demi takes a deep breath, trying to settle her racing heart, and her mind. She wonders if it has something to do with her father, and all the crazy bullshit that seems to keep following the family since his death last year, or if her stupid mother has gone and done something reckless to put her daughter in danger. Maybe pissed off the wrong drug lord in some foreign country somewhere. Life has been anything but normal this past year, and she tells herself that maybe this has nothing to do with her at all, but some drama from her parents that she's been sucked up into, and hopefully it will all be over with soon, and she'll be ok.

Fifteen minutes pass by before they are driving outside of town, away from any street lights, and only passing the odd side road and house in the distance. Then they are alone in the country side, pulling up the dirt driveway to the farm house that they planned to use as a hideout for the night.

It is Brandon's place, but it's actually owned in title by his step-uncle. No one else will be stopping by anytime soon though, as his uncle is in jail for a few more years and his aunt is living out of state. Brandon never stays here either, only checking in from time to time to make sure the place is still standing, or if he wants to have a fire and maybe a few loud drinks with the boys out of town, but he has an apartment in the city and prefers the busy living.

Though lately Brandon feels like all he does is work, bills and debt are always one step ahead of him, and it's almost as if he's drowning. In fact, that's why he's hatched this crazy plan; one easy job and he's set for life, or at least for a good while. He just wants to leave it all behind and live worry free.

He hasn't put a dime into the farm house since his aunt gave him the keys to it. Even so, it suits the needs of their kidnapping. They only plan to hold up there for a few hours anyway and it is reasonable enough; there is electricity and running water, a working TV, and he and Adam came out a few days prior to board up the windows tight, bring out fresh bedding and blankets and towels, and stock up on some food and drinks and toiletries. The guys felt it would be perfect for the night, and they're pretty sure they've thought of everything they'll need.

Brandon pulls up under the carport beside the kitchen door and kills the lights, and then they're engulfed by darkness this far into the country, with no city lights or nearby neighbors, and the stars and moon not quite bright enough through the cloudy night sky. Brandon hasn't even turned on the outside motion detector light by the doorway to light up their entrance.

Adam's truck is parked around back, hidden from view of any "nosy or casual" passerby's, just in case. They don't want to take any chances. They haven't been seen together anywhere publicly, and they have both been going to work and keeping up with odd jobs, friends, family, whatever they would normally be doing. Brandon has made sure they've put a lot of thought into their actions this past week as well, and that's what's made him the plan man here. They do not need to draw any unneeded attention to themselves, just in case something goes wrong, and Brandon is covering all of the bases.

After Brandon kills the engine, total silence fills the van for a moment and Demi catches her breath in anticipation of what's to come next. They have been driving for a while, and she can't even imagine where they may have taken her. She doesn't know if they are still in the city or if they are somewhere in the country, they drove for quite some time and she is still blindfolded and disoriented.

She hears both doors of the van open, the driver's door and the one at the back just beside her, and it slides open loudly, startling her. The guy sitting on the van floor next to her shuffles out and places his arms around her, one arm tucked under her legs grabbing her by her soft shins, and he slides her out with him, still wrapped up in the blanket. "I'm armed, so I wouldn't scream if I were you," he says softly to her in her ear, holding her tightly against him. This is not the same guy who carried her to the vehicle, she could tell instantly. His arms are holding her differently and the body she is pressed up against feels broader, plus he doesn't smell like that cheap cologne. He just smells like a man.

She feels them begin to move again, that familiar bouncing feeling and the sound of gravel crunching under foot, across the driveway and up a few stairs. Brandon holds the door open, and Adam carries her through as Brandon locks it behind them. Adam is reminded of a cartoon where the groom carries his bride across the threshold in the same manor, except knocking her head into the door frame by accident. He has to stop himself from chuckling out loud. Where had that thought even come from? It's not like he'd be carrying his bride in with a hood tied over her face and her hands bound, though the crazy thought gives him a half a chub, and he tells himself to be serious. This is no time for comic relief.

The guys walk down the hall to the living room door and Brandon unlocks that too and lets Adam in first; they have really taken no chances here, everything is double locked or boarded up tight, they only unlock one door at a time, and they each have a set of keys. Adam walks across the living room and deposits her on one of the pull-out couches while Brandon locks the door again behind them.

Demi feels rough fabric of an old couch against the back of her legs as he sits her down, and then she feels and hears one of them sit down beside her. By the smell of cologne, it wasn't the one that had just carried her into the house. It is crazy how much her other senses have begun to intensify since she's lost her sight for a while.

She feels the guy beside her shift again and her whole-body tenses at what she's imagining is about to come next.

Brandon presses his gun against her side and she recoils, pulling her arms into her stomach and curling her legs up underneath her; she knows now that they are both armed, and clearly, they mean business. She still doesn't know what they want from her, and a scared little moan escapes her clenched lips.

"Neither of us plan to hurt you," he begins, "but you've been kidnapped. We've left a ransom note at your house for your mother to find when she returns home after you don't pick her up from the airport in the morning." He waits for a minute, giving her a chance to absorb this information. "Can I take this hood off of you and trust that you won't do anything crazy? You're in the middle of nowhere in a tightly secured house with a couple of armed men," he says this as he gently nudges her with his gun again, "so that wouldn't really be advisable anyway."

She takes a moment to think about what he just said. Her brain is spinning, and she takes a few deep breaths to try to calm herself. She has so many questions running through her mind. They are her kidnappers, and they don't actually mean her any harm, or so they say, but they *are* armed, so she may as well do as they tell her as she doesn't imagine that she has any other choice. These guys are just more people looking for a piece of her family's money pie. Damn her parents, she thinks angrily, she's been right all along; this has nothing to do with her at all! Just another time in her life that she's been dragged through hell because of them.

When she finally nods, accepting that she really has no other choice right now, he pulls the hood off of her and she blinks and squints for a moment against the harsh light of the living room, feeling blinded. After sleeping and then waking up to the darkness of the hood over her face, it takes her a few moments to adjust and get her bearings. When she can finally see, she takes a good look around at her surroundings.

Demi finds herself sitting in a dingy living room on one of two ugly 1980's style looking couches in what seems to be an old run-down farm house. There are four doors that attach to the living room, three are open and one is shut, and all the windows she can see are boarded up tightly. One of the doors opens to a large bedroom that's empty of all but a bed, a small back pack of sorts on the floor, and a window that is also boarded up tightly. Another door opens to a smaller closet like room with a cot up against the wall, but that one doesn't have a window. And the last one opens on a small bathroom with a stand-up shower, no window in there either. None of the doors lead to any sort of exit. The only other door is double locked with a bolt lock and she assumes that is the door that they brought her in through and the only way out. There is a coffee table and TV between the couches and a small mini fridge in the corner. A garbage can sits beside the fridge, and another backpack and a couple of jackets are tossed in the corner. There is nothing else but dirt and dust. And an awfully old musty smell.

And then there are her kidnappers. She has been right in her assumption about there only being two of them. The guy sitting beside her must have been the one who first carried her from the house and then drove the van here. He's the older of the two, somewhere in his late 30s or early 40s she guesses, fairly good looking with that bad boy charming smile. He's heavily tattooed from what she can see around his t-shirt sleeves and down to his hands and around his neck, and he's the smaller built, but he's clearly in charge here by the way he's talking, laying down the rules and giving her that I mean business attitude.

The other guy is standing behind the TV, straight at attention and watching them, but he hasn't said a single word yet. He must have been the one who had brought her inside this place. He's younger than the other guy but older than her, somewhere around 30, and he's more muscular and taller than his buddy too. He is also heavily tattooed and doesn't really look thrilled with anything at the moment, standing there with his arms crossed and his gun holstered on his belt. And man, she thinks to herself, suddenly distracted, he is looking at her with a pair of killer blue eyes. Bedroom blue eyes. She feels her stomach clench for a moment, filled with a tingling like butterflies when they make eye contact, and she forces herself to look away.

Demi turns her attention back to the guy sitting next to her on the couch. She eyes the gun he's pointing at her, and then she can't help herself anymore, she needs to know what's going to happen next. "So, what are you planning to do then, if you aren't going to hurt me? What do you want from me? How much money do you want from us? What are your names? Where AM I?" She starts to freak out as the words just start to bubble out of her, and she forces herself to look away from the gun as she feels panic arising. She bites her tongue and clamps her mouth shut, stopping herself from asking anymore questions.

Brandon lets out a small laugh and tells her to relax and to not ask so many questions. He sets his gun down beside him on the couch, away from her reach, and begins to undo the cuffs around her wrists. Adam uncrosses his arms and unholsters his own gun and aims it at her. He clearly doesn't trust her and is taking zero chances. She feels her stomach clench again when she looks at him and makes herself keep her eyes locked on the guy sitting beside her.

"Well," says the older one beside her, "firstly, we are not going to tell you our names, that would be ridiculous. You are lucky we took the hood off of you, and you can see our faces, but we aren't monsters and we plan to be so far away from this place by tomorrow that it won't even matter. Besides, neither you or your mother are going to go to the cops anyway. Your mother is going to come home to find our note, and she's going to panic in such a desperation to get her poor only daughter back that I bet she'll race to call the number we left that's going to redirect her to our ghost phone. You are going to confirm to her that you've been kidnapped, and we will give her the information to wire money to us. Easy peasy. I am expecting she'll be so happy to have her only daughter home she'll pay any price. Once that is done, my buddy and I will drop you off at a public location and let her know where you are. Done and done. Honestly, I think the whole thing will go off without a hitch and we can have you home by lunch time. Then my buddy and I will be lost on a beach a day or so after that. Good bye shitty life!" Brandon chuckles and sits back on the couch as she's no longer cuffed, and he tosses them onto the table. He looks pleased with himself.

Demi rubs her wrists where the restraints were, then pulls the blanket even closer around her, trying to hide herself into the couch. She takes a few moments to think about everything he's just said. These guys have clearly put a LOT of thought into this, they were right; they likely aren't going to hurt her or rape her, they just want some of her old man's money like everyone else. Except they sure got one thing wrong, she isn't her mother's darling daughter, and while she'll pay any money to get her back alright, it would be to save her own face and reputation more than anything else. She doesn't care about Demi.

She lets out a small meek laugh, taking the guys by surprise. "I don't even think my mother is going to care that you've kidnapped me," she says, "ever since my father died last year she's been off drinking and partying and living up the life of a rich widow. She's going to be too busy with her men and her fun to even notice that I'm gone, other than I won't be there to be her chauffeur from the airport... But don't worry, I know she'll do as you say and pay you every cent that you ask for, just to make sure no one ever finds out about this. She's all about her reputation. But I gotta tell you, like everyone else who has come crawling out of the wood work, you're just going to be another page in her cheque book. This won't matter to her. Just like me." She looks down at the blanket as she says this last part, fidgeting with the seams of it and looking embarrassed.

Adam and Brandon exchange glances, they aren't really sure what to say in response to her sad little outburst. Adam feels the pain in her words, and he sees the way her eyes change, how they become broken, almost dead inside when she speaks about her mother like that. He remembers all too well finding his own mother drunk and passed out on many occasions as a child; missing dinner, missing him, and his sister, missing everything. The amount of times child services was in and out of his life was unbelievable and inexcusable growing up; but they never did much for him. Nor for his sister, who he was always trying to shelter and take care of. His father had left before he had more than a few memories of him, his mother didn't have much family, and Child Services didn't really have room for them in the system but didn't want to split them up either. So as long as they didn't end up beaten or malnourished, which somehow, he managed to make sure they didn't, the system left them right where they were. Alone, sad and scared. Desperate for love and a normal life. With

Adam taking care of someone else long before he was prepared to even take care of himself.

Adam remembers all too well the feelings of missing family, of longing for something better, of not belonging anywhere, just floating through life, and he curses himself for allowing those feelings to bubble up now simply because some pretty girl said something that tugged on his heart strings. Once again, he finds himself feeling terrified that he's going to let his sexual frustration or his awful control of his emotions ruin this for them; he has got to get a hold of himself.

Adam has somehow let girls screw up everything for him throughout his entire life. He does things he knows he shouldn't, things he's not comfortable with or doesn't want to do, just to make women happy or to impress them and make them like him. He lets girls hurt him over and over and break his heart and string him along, lie to him, abuse him and leave him hanging. He's developed an awful insecurity about females, and such an instant lack of trust and respect for almost any woman that comes into his life. It makes him angry that he's caught in this self-made cycle, but it's become a habit for him, and one he doesn't know how to break.

Adam snaps out of his thoughts as Brandon continues to talk. He doesn't know how to address what she's said, so he skips over it and continues on from where he stopped talking before. "Well, in any case, that's the plan. For now, we've got a handful of hours until morning and it's time to get this show on the road. Until then we've made a nice little place for you to sleep over there," as he gestures to the smaller bedroom, "and we have lots of food and drinks should you feel hungry or thirsty. We aren't hit men or anything, and we don't mean to harm you, provided you don't do anything crazy like try to attack us or run away. So, feel free to get what you need and use the washroom whenever you need to as well." With that,

Brandon gets up and walks to the mini fridge, grabs himself a beer and cracks it open. He turns to Demi and waves a soda and his beer at her, and she gestures to the beer. He puts the soda back and grabs her a beer. Shutting the fridge, he walks over to her and hands her the beer and then sits back down on the couch beside her where he was before.

As Brandon grabs the TV remote and clicks on the TV, Adam snaps to and realizes that he hasn't moved from the spot where he's been standing since they came in with her and he deposited her on the couch; he's still standing straight legged, tense, and he's also still got his gun aimed at the two of them. He needs to get it together. Brandon gives him a funny raised eyebrow look, sharing his feelings, and Adam holsters his gun, follows suit in grabbing himself a beer and he sits down on the opposite couch. He's just been so thrown by everything that's happening, and it's all happening so fast, he hadn't realized she'd be so beautiful, and clearly fucked up just like he is. He hadn't truly realized quite how badly his feelings and emotions are out of his control either. He just hadn't been expecting any of this. He tries to relax as he drinks his beer. It's only for a few more hours, he tells himself. Then he can forget all about this, and women for a while, and get his shit together while starting a whole new life.

A few minutes pass as the three of them sit there quietly watching TV. This late at night, Brandon has only managed to find an old western for them to watch, and it's not keeping anyone's attention. The silence in the room is slightly awkward, but it isn't terribly uncomfortable either; she knows now that the guys don't mean her any harm, provided she doesn't lose her shit, and she currently has no plans to do so. Also, despite what she had said about her mother, she knows that she'll come to her rescue in the morning, and this will all be done and over with. She can't kill her curiosity about how all of this ended up happening though, and she waits until she feels like an alright moment to ask, although she isn't very classy about it.

"So, how the heck did you guys end up kidnapping me, anyway?"

As far as vague parts of the background story go, Brandon has no qualms in sharing with her how he had come up with this plan in the first place. He knew a guy that used to work for her father before he passed away. He had told Brandon that Demi's mother is a rich widow who's always traveling out of the country, and that Demi's a young loner who still lives at home and was a prime candidate for a kidnapping.

Demi feels herself blush a little at being spoken about so casually, but she bites her tongue, letting the guy continue. "Right now," he says, "my life is a financial and over all mess and I need to make some drastic changes, and fast. This seems like an easy yet harmless route in the big scheme of things. Once this is done I am leaving this place, long gone, saying goodbye to my entire crappy life. It's time for me to start over fresh somewhere on a warm beach with a new name where no one knows me, and I don't owe everyone and their mamma. I'm ready for a whole new life." Brandon lifts his empty beer can into the air in a cheers motion, lets out a laugh, and gets up to grab another beer.

She turns her attention towards the younger one. He still hasn't spoken a single word to them this entire time, he's just been sitting there quietly nursing his beer and watching TV. The truth is though, he has been listening to everything. He just hasn't trusted himself to speak up yet. He's still shocked and surprised that he's been moved by Demi talking about her mother, and her life, and he can't stop looking at her long pale legs that keep peeking out from under the blanket every time she shifts around. He's totally captivated by her, and this isn't good. He feels very out of control with everything, but then again, when is he ever in control of himself around women?

Adam feels like his insides are in turmoil. This is torture for him, lost in a situation that he's supposed to be the boss in. When Demi asks him what his role in all this is, it takes him a few moments to get himself together enough to think of an answer for her. Demi isn't sure this younger guy is even going to talk to her at all. Then he does, giving her an answer that's brief and to the point. "My life hasn't been easy, I can't seem to hold down a job, and I am in a shit ton of debt. I'm in trouble with everyone right now except the law, but maybe that's only a matter of time for me too. My buddy here said it, this seems like an easy job. So, I'm just along for the ride. I just want a chance to start over with a new life too."

Demi's quiet for a moment, and then she just can't help herself. She lets out a laugh and makes a smart-ass comment which she instantly wishes that she could take back. "Seems like you both just need a couple of smart women in your lives to settle you guys down and put you back on the straight and narrow path." She hears Adam snort in response to this on the opposite couch, but Brandon just roars with laughter beside her, smacking his knee and throwing his head back. She's offended by his response, she wasn't trying to be funny, and she impatiently waits for him to explain himself. When he's done laughing, Brandon replies in an almost condescending tone, "*Us men* know that women are so much more trouble than they are actually worth, hands down. Trust me, most of the mess behind me has to do with women and if either of us still had a woman in our lives right now, we would be doing far stupider shit then kidnapping someone."

Now Adam is laughing, this turn of conversation has totally broken the fog he's been sitting in. Demi can't believe these guys, and she lets out a snort. "You cannot be serious." This time it's Adam that replies to her, and he isn't short and brisk with her anymore either. He sounds heated, mad and passionate all rolled in one. She finds she's drawn to the sound of his voice, it's deep and emotional, and commands attention. "The women in my life have caused me to lose jobs and lose the relationships I had with my friends and family. They have lied to me, cheated on me, stolen from me, and left me with even less than I started with. I've been humiliated enough from having women in my life. I'm done being blinded by pussy, I need to be in control of things again. So, I'm good. Thanks." Adam shuts up, feeling embarrassed and unsure of where that rant had even come from.

Suddenly everything gets awkward for a moment, and then Brandon breaks out into a fit of laughter and cheers' Adams little vent session. Demi is completely offended by the two of them and instantly feels herself tense up, sitting with her legs tightly crossed underneath her, the blanket clenched in her balled-up fists. She's totally prepared to defend herself and her sex. "It's not that easy for us women either you know. There's all these double standards we have to try and uphold. You guys can go and sleep with tons of women and you're a super star. We go and sleep with even a few men, and we're a slut. You want super kinky sex with a girl, but balk the minute *she* offers it if you happen to like her, because sluts don't make a good house wife, right? So, *us women* are always so torn trying to be everything, doing whatever works to figure out what you want, constantly changing what doesn't work, sometimes being shamed for our sexual appetite and sometimes being loved for it, meanwhile you guys fuck us and chuck us the same way you do last nights used jerk off rag. You're driving us crazy, and we're driving ourselves crazy over it too."

Now it's the guys turn to look at her like she's nuts, and so Demi cheers herself with her own drink, and gives their silence a little laugh. "Like you guys are the only ones with stupid relationship issues, maybe we should just all choose to be celibate," she says. Brandon is in tears now from laughter, wiping at his face and holding his sides. When he finally calms himself down, he says "You know, you are far too young to know anything about real relationships yet, so maybe we should agree to disagree until you get a little older and have a little more experience under your belt, oh, and skip the celibacy." Brandon winks at her, showing her that he's joking, but she is still almost offended by this. She takes a deep breath and bites her tongue instead, keeping her mouth shut and choosing to pick her battles wisely. If this guy wants to act like he's some old man who's 50 years her senior instead of maybe seven to ten, that's fine by her.

Adam keeps staring at her out of the corner of his eye, and he can't help feeling completely dumbfounded by her. He doesn't know what kind of girl this is in front of him anymore. She'd totally shocked him when she blurted out all of that stuff about her sex life and what guys want vs what they get, and damned if he isn't turned on by her and her long sexy legs all over again too. Would this kidnapping never end? He is so ready for this torture to be done and over with. He clearly had no idea what he was getting into when he jumped aboard with Brandon's crazy scheme, but he was not expecting this.

As if he's reading Adam's mind, Brandon gets up and shuts the TV off a few moments later at a commercial break and announces that it's time they all turn in and call it a night. Adam feels an intense amount of relief at hearing this. It's almost over. The older one gestures to the bathroom and tells her that she can have a few minutes to wash up and use the facilities and then he'll be showing her to her room.

Demi takes a deep breath and gets up; she's going to do as she's told and not press her luck. She's also feeling relieved that it's time for bed. The night has passed fairly quickly for her and she is ever so grateful the guys have kept their word; she's going to bed untouched and by morning she will be going home unharmed. That's all she wants right now, is to go home. She's getting a crazy sexual vibe from the younger one, with those deep blue intense eyes, plus she's confused, a little scared, emotional and exhausted, and she's ready for all of this to be over with.

She heads to the bathroom and washes her face quickly, then uses the toilet and she's back out again in under five minutes, ready for bed. She's still wearing the nightie she was in when they grabbed her from her house, and she feels both exposed and a little girlish in her outfit. She follows Brandon across the living room to the doorway of the smaller closet like bedroom, avoiding making eye contact with the younger guy entirely. Every time she looks at him, her stomach seems to tie itself into knots. She doesn't understand it, but there's something about him, whether it's his looks or something else she can't quite put her finger on, she's simply drawn to him and she doesn't like it.

Brandon stands there in the doorway watching her closely as she crosses the living room, and he opens his arms to give her a mock grand entrance when she gets to the bedroom, acting very charming like." Your room awaits my dear." "Some digs," she replies sarcastically, "good thing I'm not claustrophobic." She hears the younger one snort on the couch behind her, but she refuses to turn around. Brandon doesn't have a reply for this either; instead, he waves the gun from her to the bedroom and back again, and she enters willingly. He hands her a bottle of water, then shuts the door behind her and locks her in. He turns to Adam and says with a laugh, "She's just lucky I didn't cuff her up in there. That would have been a hell of a sleep."

The guys don't talk too much after that; Brandon uses the washroom first and then retires into the larger empty bedroom. As it's his place and he's the mastermind here, Brandon takes the actual bedroom to sleep in while Adam gets his pick of either two pull outs in the living room. Adam isn't going to complain though, Brandon didn't have to invite him along or give him a decent cut of the pay, he probably could have pulled this whole thing off himself somehow. Aside from the sexual tension between him and Demi, this will be the easiest job Adam has ever done, and definitely the most well paid. That makes it worth all the aggravation to him.

It isn't long before Adam can hear Brandon snoring loudly through the partially closed doorway. It isn't shut all the way, just in case something happens out here. Adam slides the coffee table and TV out of the way, and then pulls out one of the couches and makes himself a bed. He lays there for a long time afterwards, listening to Brandon snore, listening to Demi shuffle around on her cot, and lost in his own thoughts, driving himself crazy.

The past day has been a wild whirlwind for him. All of the planning they had put into this, and timing everything out perfectly had been stressful enough, but waiting is the worst. This anticipation of not knowing what's going to come is driving him insane, he's just hoping everything goes according to Brandon's plan.

Actually pulling off the kidnapping itself has been the scariest and most thrilling rush he's had in his life so far, and that's saying a lot. Then the rest of the nights events unfolded unlike anything he could have imagined; getting her here, seeing her, listening to her talk... It seems ridiculous to admit it, but he is unbelievably turned on by her, from who she is inside, to seeing her sexy naked legs poking out of the blanket, to seeing her and carrying her cuffed and helpless.

Adam sighs quietly to himself. He has got to change this course of thinking before he gets himself carried away. He forces his mind to think about the morning instead, and what lies ahead for them. Brandon swears the whole thing is going to go off without a hitch and they'll be safe in terms of police and jail. Demi certainly seems to think that her mother isn't going to go to the police because she won't want anyone to know what's had happened to her darling daughter. And that's a good thing for Adam, because he does not feel like he'd do well in jail, and so far in his life he's been lucky to avoid it. But if he's honest with himself, this whole thing just seems too easy, and maybe it is to someone like Brandon who is that much more in control of himself. Adam's tried to mention problems in the plan, and what ifs to Brandon before this, but Brandon shot him down. Nothing can go wrong, he said. Adam wonders if it really *will* all work out as planned; drop the girl, split the money and then take off and start a new life.

Brandon's already bought his train ticket for tomorrow night and he's got a plan for where he's going to go and what he's going to do next, but Adam feels so lost. He was already so lost before all of this with Demi started too; a million dollars is a lot of money, and all he's actually been able to think about. Once they pull this off, he really truly will be able to start over again. He hasn't given it any real thought past that; his apartment is still furnished with all of his belongings, and he even has food and beer in his fridge. He knows one thing though, after all of this is over with he isn't going to be able to stay here, in this small town, not after the kidnapping of those sexy little legs in the other room. He's not going to want the reminder of her, or her legs. Oh, but what he wouldn't give to crawl between them, spread them wide and have his way with her.

Demi tosses and turns in the small bedroom on the tiny cot, desperately trying to get herself comfortable. Her mind is racing, and she tries to calm it, listening to the sounds of the pull-out bed squeak in the other room as one of the other guys tosses and turns too. She draws comfort from the thought that she's clearly not the only restless sleeper here tonight. She imagines it's the younger one, as the older guy seems to be in charge and would have likely taken the big bedroom, and he also seems sure enough of himself that he's probably sleeping like a baby.

She finds herself going over the last few hours of her life; being kidnapped is a very surreal feeling for her, but she feels she is relatively safe. The guys have made it clear they have no intentions of hurting her and they haven't laid a finger on her yet, in fact they've been very hospitable and kind, and that's helped eliminate the feelings she should be having right now, like terror and uncertainty. She could do without the cot though, and she imagines the pullouts in the living room are probably even comfier than this, as old and musty as they look. These guys just want the ransom money from her mother and she knows they'll get it. Her mother would never allow word of this to get out to anyone, and she certainly has plenty of money to spare. This will all be over with soon.

As she's thinking about everything, she finds herself wondering how she's even in this predicament in the first place, and suddenly she can't understand herself or her actions of late, now that she's looking at things from fresh eyes and a different perspective. Why is she still living with her mother? She is a grown ass woman. She shouldn't have even been there to be kidnapped at all. Yes, they're both still hurting badly from her father's death, but deep down she knows that's just an excuse to not have to move on and be alone.

Her and her mother are healing and dealing with everything in such very different ways from each other anyway. Demi isn't getting the love or affection that she needs from her mother right now, and she never really did, living there just seems to be her way of having someone around. Except her mother's always gone anyways and she *is* always alone. Her mother doesn't inquire about how her therapy is going, or what's happening in her personal life, or even why she's still living at home at 26 years old. It's time she takes some of the money she's got put aside and goes traveling, especially after this whole kidnapping has opened her eyes. She almost snorts to herself, thinking how dumb it is that it's taken some crazy life changing experience to make her realize she isn't a pathetic teenager anymore, and that it's time to move on with her life.

Thinking of the kidnapping again brings her thoughts back to reality, and back to the kidnappers, and more specifically the one who is still awake in the other room, squeaking and rolling around on the pull out. She finds herself hoping, again, that it's the younger one with the gorgeous yet troubled eyes, a killer body, and such sexy ink. She starts dreaming about those cuffs again, and being taken against her will, and about how oddly erotic she finds this whole situation, as weird as those thoughts are to be having in a time like this.

Demi starts thinking about what it would have been like if it was the younger one taking her, all alone instead of with his buddy, and she fantasizes about him cuffing her and throwing her over his shoulder and taking her to his place instead. As her mind begins to race in a hundred different directions, some sexy and some not, a light bulb goes off inside of her, and she finds herself thinking: if she got the chance, maybe she could seduce the younger one, come on to him, make out with him, sneak his keys out of his pocket and then run away the moment he takes his eyes off of her. Then she'd never have to be rescued by her mother and dragged through all this family bullshit. She could save herself. It wasn't exactly a plausible plan, there are two guys after all, not just one, and they are armed as well, but it's one hell of a sexy thought and so she lets her mind run with it, imagining how it would happen here.

She could find a way to get the two of them alone first thing in the morning, maybe they could get the older one to go out for something, coffee, food, whatever. Something that would keep him away for a while. She'd get herself comfortable on the couch beside the younger one, close enough that maybe their knees would touch. She'd seen the way he looks at her, and she knew what his look did to her; there was something between them and she knew she'd be able to get his attention. Besides, girls were just whores, right? The guys hadn't argued with her on that point earlier. And why should she worry about what he thought about her coming on to him anyway? He's just her kidnapper after all.

She'd lean over him to grab her drink from the table, brushing against him, touching his leg briefly with her arm, and that soft touch would start to raise their blood pressure and the tension between them. She'd turn to look at him and that's when the spark between them would light on fire, and he'd be compelled to lean in and kiss her. He wouldn't be able to help himself, she was sure of it, with all the sexual heat between them, and her putting herself out there like that. A simple kiss is all it will take, and then they'd be all over each other. She'd slip the keys from his pocket as they kiss and touch each other, and they strip off each other clothes, but her thoughts trail away from the key and on to other things as she thinks about having his hands all over her, cupping her breasts, trailing along her smooth skin, lowering himself upon her. She is lost in the thought of having someone dominate and control her, and just take her.

She imagines him pushing her down on the couch underneath him, pinning her body with his own, kissing her neck, down her chest, biting first one nipple, and then the other. She'd moan and push her body against his, but he'd take that as a sign that she was trying to escape, so he'd reach out and grab the cuffs from the coffee table beside them and he'd cuff her wrist to the side of the table in one smooth motion. He'd keep kissing her deeply to stifle her fake moans of protest. He'd use his hands and mouth to have his way with her and take her while she was cuffed, and she'd be pushing back against him and pulling against her restraints, eager for more. Eventually he'd be rock hard and more than willing to lay across her again and pin her down and this time fill her with his aching cock. Maybe taking a leg up over his shoulder and forcing himself deeper inside of her as he pushes her into the couch. Filling her roughly. Pinning her down. Taking her.

Her fantasy is far too much for her, and her heart is racing wildly as she comes back down to reality. She is soaked in her own juices and horny beyond belief. Timidly, feeling slightly awkward at the situation but too needy now to care, Demi reaches down between her legs and pushes her fingers against her panties, finding them drenched. She moans softly and slips her fingers underneath the fabric, sliding her soft folds apart and lightly rubbing her clit, thrusting against her hand. She imagines Adam taking her harder, faster, filling her, fucking her, pinning her down and making her his. She starts to cum for real as her imagination sees the two of them cumming together on the pull-out couch, hot and sweaty, her pulling against the cuffs as he lies with his weight on top of her, breathing heavy.

She lays there on the bed after, coming back to the real world, silently gasping for air and feeling her heart beat begin to slow down. It dawns on her that instead of imagining a more plausible seducing escape plan, all she's done is have one hell of a hot sexual fantasy. And while the orgasm was nice, it's just another orgasm, and she is getting tired of only getting them when she gives them to herself. She could almost laugh, but instead a long heavy sigh escapes her as reality comes crashing back down around her more clearly now. She's kidnapped, truly kidnapped and taken hostage style, and she'll wait here for her mother to rescue her in the morning. This is no fantasy world she's in, and there will be no rescuing herself.

Demi feels herself grow sad at this thought, and tries to get comfortable on the cot, preparing herself for bed. She rolls over and over for a while, an absolute mess, and then begins a slow descent into a troubled and restless sleep filled with bad dreams.

Adam isn't doing much better himself. His mind is racing, but it's constantly taking him back to those long sexy legs underneath her short tiny nightie, it's girlish and adds to her look of helplessness. He also can't stop thinking about the way she looked all tied up and vulnerable in the back of the van, and oh man how much he would kill to see the two of those combined together in his favor; her tied up and willing, half naked and totally his for the taking. He'd love to crawl between her legs and dominate her and make her cum and cum and cum. He can hear the bed squeaking under her weight in there as she rolls around and around, and he can't stop picturing her rolling around underneath *him*, pressing her hot naked body up against his, so soft and warm and eager for him. He feels himself grow hard in his jeans, he's been hard on and off all night, and precum soaks the inside of his boxers. He can't seem to get a handle on himself, and he needs to get her out of his mind.

He's almost got himself calmed down and relaxed enough to sleep when he swears he hears her moan from behind the bedroom door. That's all it takes, and he's rock solid again, his cock throbbing, aching to be stroked by her, or more honestly buried in her tight wet pussy. He can't take it anymore, and he knows that the awfully loud rusty pull out is no place for a jerk off. He does not need to be waking anyone up.

Sheepishly, Adam gets up and heads to the bathroom, eyes darting from bedroom door to bedroom door, and he shuts and locks himself inside to relieve himself to thoughts of the girl they had kidnapped with long sexy pale legs. The girl he's imagining cuffed up and his for the taking. It doesn't take him long, a few slow strokes, then speeding up and gripping himself tightly while thinking about being deep inside her tight wet folds, taking her, pinning her, with her moaning beneath him.

When he's finished he washes up and quietly returns to the pull out. Then just like Demi, Adam begins an anxious tossing and turning game that eventually leads to a short and restless sleep before dawn.

Chapter Three:
Sunday Morning

Brandon is the first of the trio to wake up. Unlike the other two, he's at peace with himself and his decisions, and he doesn't carry the sexual tension or anxiety that Adam or Demi do either. He slept well and restful, knowing that this is his day to finally change his life. He almost jumps out of bed he's so bright eyed and chipper with excitement, eager to get the day started. He's set his alarm so that they'll all be awake and ready with plenty of time once her mother gets herself home and finds the ransom note, and then still ended up waking up long before it went off. There will be no excuses.

He dresses and wanders out into the living room area quietly and then into the bathroom, being careful not to wake Adam yet, or their kidnapped princess in the other room. He takes a few minutes to use the washroom and freshen up. When he's done he leaves the living room just as quietly and makes his way to the kitchen to start a pot of coffee, mentally going through the day ahead, ecstatic that things will be getting started soon. He has his train ticket tucked into the extra bag of luggage that he's got hidden away in the back of his van; tonight, once this is over, he'll take that along with the bag he's got here in the house with him and hit the road. Shortly after that, he will be long gone out of this town. Peace out, see ya later, no thanks for the awful memories.

He feels it would be a lot safer to catch a red eye flight from the airport in another city instead of from here, this is just too small of a town and people always talk. If people *are* going to talk about him, he wants them to talk about how he was just gone one day, and not, "I saw Brandon leave on an airplane to such and such place." Once he's landed safely overseas, he'll cash in his bank account and live on the beach. Brandon doesn't dream big, or lavishly. He dreams of comfort and an easier life.

He doesn't think Adam has put much thought into what he plans to do after this is over though, but Brandon keeps telling himself that Adam is no longer his problem by tonight. Friends or not, it is time for Brandon to start thinking about himself and worrying about himself, no one else. It's time to make Brandon his #1 priority. The opposite of that is why his life has fallen apart in the first place.

Once the coffee's brewed, he puts the pot and three mugs plus a bowl of sugar and a cup of creamer on a tray and brings it back to the living room, shutting and locking the doors behind him. He's still lost in thought, thinking about how easy it'll be to just drop off the girl and sail right on through, leave his run down old van at the train station and say goodbye to everything. He has a new ID already set, it pays to know people, and although it's not perfect it will last for now. He won't have any need for ID once he gets where he's planning on going.

He isn't expecting any trouble anyway. No cops, no jail time, not with this family. He's been doing research for weeks prior to this, and he knows the girl's mother is all about keeping face. This will be a simple exchange between him and the mother for money and her daughter this afternoon, and then it'll be over with after that. If all Adam wants to do is go back to his shit ass apartment and mope, sitting on a million dollars, that's fine, but Brandon isn't sticking around to find out. He has had enough of this life, and this is his opportunity to change that.

Brandon finds Adam stirring on the pull out when he returns, and he's sure he hears movement on that old springy cot in the closet bedroom. He sets the tray of coffee down on the table between the couches and gives Adam a shake, fully arousing him from his slumber. Adam nods at him, and Brandon nods his head in return towards the coffee tray. There doesn't need to be a lot of words used this early in the morning. There hasn't been a lot of sleeping lately, and coffee is about all they need.

Brandon walks over to the small bedroom and knocks on the door a few times to make sure that Demi is awake. When he hears her make a faint reply, he lets her know that he's unlocking the door and she's welcome to come out once she's more awake. "The washroom is free and there's a mug of coffee out here with your name on it too." He says to the closed door.

Brandon walks over to the couch across from the pull out and sits down, and he and Adam begin to put their morning mugs of coffee together, passing the sugar and cream back and forth. There still isn't much chatter between them. Adam looks drained and exhausted. Brandon takes the ghost phone out of his pocket and places it on the table beside the tray of coffee. He is ready as ever for that thing to start ringing and for this to all be over with.

Demi sits on the cot for a few minutes before she gets up, not sure how ready she is to start this day, even though she's desperate to go home. She opens the door slowly, peeks out, and then sheepishly takes off across the room for the bathroom while struggling to keep her nightie pulled down over her ass. She's still feeling rather ashamed of the way she had turned this whole situation into some sort of sexual fantasy last night, even if there was no way that the guys would ever know, and right now running across the living room with her ass jiggling like this makes her feel like she's still the star in her 3am porno. Her face is burning, and she's quick to shut the bathroom door and hide herself away for a few more minutes.

Adam almost chokes on his coffee, sitting there half awake, watching her bum peek out from the bottom of her tiny nightie as she hurries by. He too is remembering his thoughts from the night before, and his shameless act in the bathroom. He must have blushed or made some sort of noise, because he looks up from his mug to find Brandon giving him a dirty look and shaking his head at him. "Adam," he says, "We shouldn't have to talk about this, *again*, but we will. You are a nut when it comes to women and you have gotta keep that shit in check right now. A fine ass is *not* worth risking millions over. You should be smart enough to know that man. And she is *not* sitting around in that nightie until her mother calls, so why don't you do us both a favor, even if you may not see it as such, and rummage her up something to cover herself with. Your clothes will fit her far better than anything of mine ever will anyway. Although I will say, those legs of hers are very nice. I can't blame you *too* much for seeing them as a distraction."

Adam doesn't reply right away. He doesn't quite trust himself to do so. A part of him is pissed off at Brandon for putting him on the spot, and part of him is pissed off at himself because he knows that Brandon is right. He was just jerking off over that girl last night in the bathroom, he *doesn't* have any self-control! He does need to get his shit together, and fast.

He nods and then gets up and digs through the bag of stuff he has stashed in the corner; both guys had thought to bring a handful of clothes and odds and ends that they weren't sure if they would need or not but wanted to have just in case. He manages to find a pair of shorts and a t shirt that he doesn't really mind parting with. He tosses them at

Brandon and lets him handle it, Adam just doesn't want to be the one to bring her his clothes to wear.

Brandon takes them to the bathroom door, knocks on it and tells her that he has a change of clothes for her for now, so that she doesn't need to feel so exposed sitting around in her nightie. The door opens a crack and her hand snakes out, grabs the clothes from him and then she shuts the door again just as quickly, and he hears a mumbled thank you come from behind the door. Brandon lets out a laugh. Clearly, she is just as anxious to be covered up as his buddy is to see her naked. Though, he has to admit, he really wouldn't mind the view himself.

He returns back to the couch and the guys sip their coffee while Demi gets dressed. They still aren't talking much, feeling excitement mixed in with some tension and stress, all of them anxious for the morning to really start.

When Demi comes out of the washroom a few minutes later and takes a seat on the couch beside Brandon and across from the couch Adam's on, he practically jumps up and heads in to the washroom for his turn to get ready, not eager to see her again yet, and especially not eager to see her in his clothes. She's wearing clothes he wore only a few days ago and having her wear them is doing something to him that he doesn't understand.

He spends a lot longer in the bathroom than he needs to, considering all he does is wash his face and brush his teeth, use the toilet, wash up and give himself a little pep talk about getting a hold of himself. He just wants to make sure that he has a handle on himself before he goes back out to join them in waiting for her mother to call. He doesn't need to be saying anything dumb, or acting like a teenager, sporting a hard on every time he looks at her.

Once he's finally ready, he exits to see that Brandon has tucked the pull-out bed away for him and tidied up, and that he and Demi are sitting together back on the couch opposite where he was sitting before, which gives Adam the couch he slept on all to himself. Well, he thinks, not having to sit beside her is a good thing. Although the clothes he's given to her to wear are absolutely killing him, and for a lot of reasons that's a bad thing. The shorts are far too baggy and end up showing a lot more of her long legs than that damn nightie did. The t-shirt is also far too large for her, and the neck area keeps sliding off her shoulder, and as it slips it exposes more and more of her smooth bare skin. She is constantly fidgeting with it, pulling his shirt tightly around her, and he can't help but think that if she were to lean over or bend forward at all, he'll be able to see right down it. And she isn't wearing anything underneath it either, he knows that. This broad is going to be the death of him, he's already sporting the half chub he swore to himself he wouldn't have all morning.

He takes a seat on the empty couch and picks his coffee back up, feeling a little awkward thanks to his run-away emotions. Brandon and Demi are making small talk with each other, but he can't seem to get into what they're talking about, and instead he watches the TV throw images in front of his eyes. He can't seem to make himself pay attention or focus on anything around him. Just looking at her is too much for him. He is dying for this to be over with, he already feels like he is in over his head. Nothing that he's experiencing, or feeling is what he signed up for, he was not expecting anything like this. He's ready to secure the cash, drop the girl off and.... Well, Adam doesn't know what comes after that. He's just ready for this part to be done. He needs to be away from her, out of her presence. Just the sight of her, the things that she says, her smell, she is driving him crazy and becoming an awful sore spot for him. His lack of self-control and all of his stupid emotions are going to ruin him.

Chapter Four:
Sunday, just after breakfast

Adam is the first one to start getting a little twitchy when the phone doesn't ring 5 minutes after Demi's mother's plane lands. He tries to tell himself he's being irrational; between flight delays, baggage claim, her mother waiting around to make sure Demi isn't coming, calling the house, calling for a cab, and then finally getting home and finding their note, it could take her mother a few extra hours to find out about the kidnapping and call the ghost phone. Still, he has been watching the clock almost constantly, and with every second that ticks by he grows more and more anxious for something to happen.

He knows he needs to kick this stress before it starts to consume him, because this is stupid. He tries to focus back in on what the other two are chatting about, and he hears Brandon and Demi talking about some movie that's being made from a book. It's so casual and so out of sorts from all the anxiety and sexual stress that he's feeling, and Adam can't take it anymore. He grabs the coffee pot without saying a word, unlocks the living room door and locks it behind him as he goes through, and then heads to the kitchen to make another pot of coffee.

Right now, he's so irritated by the casual chatter going on between the other two, he's too turned on by everything she does and says, and he can't seem to be able to control himself. He needs to keep busy until this is over. He's too tired and restless from not sleeping the night before, and from lack of sleep preparing the few nights before that, and the phone not ringing when it's supposed to is driving him up the wall and getting on his last nerve. Plus, he just wants to pin her down and bury himself inside of her. All in all, it won't be long before he snaps from the pressure. He makes the second pot of coffee of the day and checks the wall clock one more time as he walks back down the hallway to the living room and locks up behind himself again.

When he enters the living room, he notices that the mood in the room has changed. His tension seems to have spread, and he is no longer the only one stressed and anxious. Brandon has the TV turned to the news now, and Adam can only assume it's because they are keeping an eye out for word of her kidnapping. The thought causes a knot to form in the pit of his stomach. Could Brandon have been wrong about the police? Time has been passing slowly, but enough time has gone by now that they are all waiting for word from her mother.

Adam sets the pot of coffee down on the tray with the sugar and creamer and takes a seat on the couch. They all pour another mug and sit in silence for a few minutes, each lost in their own thoughts. Demi breaks it with an awkward joke about how she is so unwanted, her mother probably saw the note about her being kidnapped, said good riddance and went on with her day. "She won't even have to tell anyone it happened," Demi continues, "She could just tell people that I picked up a job working overseas or something, poof, gone from her life." She finishes this off with a chuckle, but it falls flat, and sad.

The guys exchange a look similar to the one they shared last night as Demi takes a sip of coffee, eyes on the TV, avoiding looking at either of them. Even Brandon, with his hard heart, feels a little bit for her as she sits in silence watching the news. This can't be easy for her, he thinks to himself, not only would being kidnapped be scary enough, but imagine making jokes because you didn't know if your mother was really going to save you or not.

Chapter Five:
Sunday, shortly before lunch

Tick. Tock. Tick. Tock. They are all sneaking glances at the wall clock, and now every single stroke of the second hand seems like the sound of mocking laughter to Brandon. Time keeps passing and it gets closer and closer to noon. Brandon knows something has gone wrong. He begins to feel a pit of awful dread and panic forming in his stomach, almost to the point of nausea. He can't stop thinking that her mother has come home and freaked out when she saw the note; maybe she went to the cops anyway, and now there's a silent manhunt out for them. Maybe they're going to end up in jail after all. Maybe they're tracing them to the farm house right now. Maybe it's already all over.

He's starting to feel like he can't breathe. The situation just isn't going as planned, and his mind is racing out of control. He needs to get out of this room and think before his run-away thoughts take over and he snaps. Brandon has a temper, a very bad one when not kept in check, and that isn't new to him; it has gotten him in trouble many times in the past, and he knows it could do the same in this situation as well. He's been on Adam nonstop to keep his sexual shit together, well, Brandon needs to keep his temper in check too. *He* doesn't need to ruin their chances at a couple million either, especially over something a ten second breather could prevent.

Adam can tell something is up with Brandon. The passing of time has to be getting to him. Brandon has been unable to sit still for some time, instead fidgeting all over the couch. He is always the one to instigate conversation and keep things running smoothly, and yet he's just spent hours sitting tight lipped and silent. He only takes his eyes off the wall clock long enough to check on the news, and he's pale and sweaty.

Adam senses his friend is about to snap, and Brandon doesn't disappoint him. A moment later Brandon jumps up and announces he is going into the kitchen to check flight schedules and to make some phone calls. "You two can stay right here while I figure this out." He barks at them, on his way to the door. "It is getting too close to lunch, we skipped breakfast, I am starving, and this waiting game is pissing me off."

Brandon gets up and storms out of the room, not waiting for a reply from Adam and slamming the living room door behind him, locking it after. Demi and Adam find themselves sitting in an awkward silence after he's gone, with the news playing in the background. Adam can't stand the sound of the announcer's voice, it's getting on his nerves and she just keeps repeating the same news over and over anyway, irritating him even more than he already is. He forces himself to take a slow, deep breath, as he can feel his own patience fading fast at the situation at hand. Brandon's freak out seems pretty reasonable right now, but Adam can't join him.

He looks over at Demi and finds she's just sitting there, staring into her empty mug, looking tired and a little bit scared. He can't really blame her there. He takes another deep breath and calms himself a little more, knowing that having both of the guys testy will only make the situation worse for her and for them.

He doesn't want them to sit in silence anymore, between that and the tension it's more than he can bear. He doesn't know what to say to her though, so he asks her the first thing that pops into his head. "Are you doing alright?" Demi looks up at him when he speaks, startled to hear his voice, and she thinks if she'd had any coffee left in her mug, she probably would have spilled it everywhere. "That seems like a weird question to ask me, considering what's happening right now, but thank you. I guess I am doing OK." she replies, and he feels his damn heart pinch again for her and her vulnerability. After a pause, she continues. "Um, you know, I was just thinking about something a few minutes ago, and I'm not trying to tell you guys what to do or anything... but maybe you could check my cell phone, if you brought it, or call my house and see if my mother left any messages. Maybe she had to catch a different flight or something, or she changed her vacation plans, and we just don't know about it. My mother is really impulsive, and it doesn't really surprise me that she hasn't called you guys yet, but, it's very likely that she's called me in the meantime."

Now it's Adam's turn to be startled, and he feels a sudden wave of relief wash over him in response to what she's just said. It makes total sense. All of this extra waiting has been for something simple, he's sure of it, and now they will figure out what's going on, get it sorted out, and this may all still be over with by supper at the latest. And done will still be done, as Brandon would say. Adam lets out a big sigh, not realizing he's been holding his breath, and he feels some of his tension fade away. He makes eye contact with Demi and then he lets out a laugh, catching her off guard.

"Well, you know what, you're probably right. I honestly can't believe we didn't think of that before, with all of the prepping and planning that my buddy and I have put into this. And here we are, acting like we've thought of everything. Once he's back in here and we know there isn't an issue with the flights or something else, that's going to be the next step." Adam leans back on the couch, pleased with himself and with her for suggesting it, and sits there with a big grin on his face, thinking about how quick things have could have just sorted themselves out. If Brandon doesn't come back in here soon, he's just going to have to lock her in here alone and go out and tell him himself and save his friend some of the anxiety and aggravation he's bound to be going through by now.

Demi isn't so happy though. She doesn't say anything more, deciding to wait it out, but it isn't that the thought of going home doesn't make her happy. Demi honestly just doesn't think a simple flight delay is the reason that her mother isn't calling the ransom phone. She knows how truly flaky and selfish her mother can be. And she doesn't know what's going to happen if things stop going according to these guys plans. What is going to happen to her? She hates the thought of having to rely on her mother to save her.

The two of them sit in a less tense silence for a few more minutes, each of them lost in their own thoughts. Adam is trying very hard not to think about the girl sitting across from him, because he doesn't understand what he's feeling. Instead he tries to think about what he's going to do when he cashes in his million bucks. Demi is just trying not to lose herself into a depression of thoughts that are lingering just around the corners of her mind. She really doesn't know what's going on right now or what's going to happen and getting herself worked up for nothing is only going to make things worse.

A few minutes later they hear Brandon coming back down the hallway. He comes storming into the living room and slams the door behind him on his way back in again, clearly in the same mood as he was when he left. Before Adam can say anything to him, he announces loudly that the flight was on schedule, and that her mother has checked out of the hotel she was staying at already, so he doesn't have any explanation for what's happening. "I don't know any more now than I did before," he says miserably.

Brandon sits down on the couch feeling defeated. He's expecting a bunch of questions to come his way, he assumes they'll be wondering what the plan is next. But instead, it takes him right by surprise that the other two don't seem stressed by that too much at all, and don't voice any concerns. In fact, they seem to be quite relaxed, and are exchanging glances of their own like they have some sort of secret to share.

"What's going on in here," he asks, jokingly yet almost accusingly, eyeing the pair of them up. "Have you two suddenly decided that you're fine with shacking it up for an indefinite amount of time?? Because I am certainly not OK with that, no offense to both of you." Brandon finishes sarcastically. Demi feels herself blush at the thought of shacking up with the younger one, and it doesn't go unnoticed by Adam. He can't help but feel curious at her blush; does it have anything to do with him?

He forces himself to push the thought away and continue the conversation. "None taken man, I wouldn't want to be shacked up with you either. But don't be jealous, you left the room willingly," Adam replies quickly, and he gives her a wink. Now she feels like she's blushing from her face right down to her toes, she may as well be on fire; her heart is racing, and her blood is hot, this is just like last night all over again. What the hell is wrong with her? She's mortified that she's acting like some stupid school girl with her first crush and isn't able to handle herself. Demi needs to get it together. "No", Adam continues, breaking her out of her thoughts, "but in all seriousness, Demi had an idea about calling in to her cell phone and home phone and checking the messages, maybe her mother ended up taking a different flight or changing her vacation plans or something, and she called and left a message for her."

When Adam stops talking, a silence falls over the room for a moment as Brandon absorbs this, and then he laughs. It's a real laugh, and as he laughs he relaxes a bit and it helps ease the tension and stress in the room significantly. "Well, why the hell didn't we think of that sooner? Some planning we did man, and we thought we were totally prepared for everything." Brandon says, almost repeating what Adam said to Demi earlier. He chuckles a little bit more, enjoying the moment of peace he's feeling, and then he puts his business face on.

He grabs the ghost phone off of the table and asks her for the number to her cell phone first, and what he needs to do to dial into her voice mail. He isn't willing to use his personal cell phone for this and risk leaving any traceable numbers behind. Demi explains to him what he needs to do, and he dials in and listens, still chuckling to himself. He puts the phone to his ear, and within moments his laughter and good humor are gone. Both Adam and Demi can feel the tension and frustration creep back into him and into the room as he listens to the voice mail, and his face drops. Brandon's hand tightens into a fist at his side.

Demi feels her chest constrict at the look on the older one's face. She knew it, she just knew it. Something has changed with her mother's vacation plans. She's either extending her stay, moving on to somewhere else, or hell, who knows. Her mother is so spontaneous, what is she going to do if they don't get a hold of her? Who will come to rescue her? Is she going to have to rescue herself? She's scared and angry and confused, and she can feel that she's starting to panic, and doesn't know how to calm down right now.

Adam watches her face fall, and he can figure out what she is thinking easily enough. He's starting to feel the same way himself; panicked about the change in their situation, and the uncertainty of what's going to happen next. This is exactly what he tried to warn Brandon about before all this happened, this is what he wanted them to be prepared for, but that's beside the point now. Too little too late. Adam's chest grows tight, and he starts to have a hard time breathing as well. The anxiety of waiting for Brandon to hang up and say something is killing him. This whole thing has been a waiting game really. He doesn't know how much more waiting and anticipation he can take.

Brandon pulls the ghost phone away from his ear, disconnects the phone call and angrily throws it down on the table. They all watch it slide across and bounce softly into the coffee tray. Brandon's whole posture has suddenly changed; he is rigid, and his hands are now clenched tightly into fists on his knees. "Fuck." He says, and for the first time in this kidnapping, he truly feels lost and out of control.

That one word settles it for her. Demi jumps up in a panic, her whole face gone white. She's freaking out inside, knowing that something must have happened to her mother's vacation plans, and now she won't be coming for her. The thought terrifies her more than this whole kidnapping has so far, and she starts yelling at them that they have to let her out of here, they can't just keep her. "My mother isn't coming for me and this isn't fair!!" She yells out in a panic.

Demi is so lost in her self-made terror that she doesn't even notice when the older guy stands up and walks over to her. Brandon grabs her by the arm and pulls her back down onto the couch beside him, almost dragging her down. He keeps a tight grip on her arm, so hard that he almost hurts her, but he manages to break through her fog. "Listen, sweetheart," he says to her, "your mother is perfectly fine. And perfectly fucking us. But we will get all of this figured out." He makes a frustrated sound. "Urrgh! Kisses darling? Who says that though." He lets go of her now and tosses her arm away, sitting back against the couch and rubbing at his face, letting out another disgruntled sigh of disbelief and anger.

Even though she's no longer in a total freak out, it still takes Demi a minute or two to really comprehend what he's said to her about her mother. She knows exactly what "kisses darling" means. Here she is kidnapped for crying out loud, and her mother is off doing what she always does, which is being selfish and not giving a rat's ass for anyone else in the world, least of all her one and only daughter. She doesn't care about her daughter's safety, she doesn't even care how Demi does on a day to day basis, she cares more for her own happiness than anything else in the world. Demi may really be on her own here.

"So, what does that mean then," she asks, turning to the older guy and getting him to confirm what she already knows, "that she's still off enjoying her vacation? She's moved on to somewhere else? She's not coming home for me?? If so, what's going to happen to me? Can you get a hold of her? Can she still wire you money? What if you *don't* get a hold of her? What if no one comes to rescue me? Can I pay you instead? How much money are you guys asking for me?"

Brandon sighs, leaning back and putting his feet up on the coffee table and toying with the gun in his holster. He is trying not to let her nonstop questions overwhelm him, but she's almost too much for him. He is trying to brainstorm, but he's starting to feel really pissed off, and he can't concentrate with her losing her shit like this. He needs to control his mind, or make her control herself, or leave the room and do something about his temper. Because he knows that once he loses his cool, he is going to totally lose his cool. And he doesn't want to do that here. He's the one in charge, and he has to set the example of keeping things together.

"Can you just quit it? OK! Please! Stop with all of this nagging!" Brandon jumps up and kicks out at the coffee table, a little harder than he intended to, and it slides across the carpet. The contents on the table spill everywhere, and the table itself hits Adam in the shin. If they hadn't drank all the coffee dry in anticipation of the day ahead, the ghost phone may have met an unpleasant fate.

Demi feels herself begin to panic even more at the sudden turn of events. How is her mother supposed to pay for the ransom and let her go free, if she doesn't even know Demi is kidnapped at all? She's been right all along; her mother isn't coming for her. She's going to have to rescue herself. She's on her own here. And what is going to happen if this guy loses his temper, and finally snaps? And what about the younger one? Will he just let something bad happen to her? They both have guns. She starts to feel like she can't breathe, bombarding herself with all of these questions she doesn't have answers to. She needs to get out of here.

Brandon and Adam stare at each other, and Brandon looks very angry. Adam's leg is smarting from the sliding coffee table and he knows it's going to leave a good mark. He wants to say something, but he also doesn't want to say the wrong thing and set Brandon off completely, so he keeps quiet and waits for Brandon to speak first. Which he does after he takes a few deep breaths to calm his shaking voice. "You and I are going for a chat in the kitchen. *Now!* Put her in the bedroom and lock her up and then follow me."

Brandon starts to head towards the door. He, too, desperately needs to get out of this stuffy living room; his head is pounding, he can't seem to grasp everything that's happening all at once, and he can't stand to be around her panicking like this. He doesn't want to admit it, but he's feeling scared and lost about what to do now too, and he's mad at himself for not taking Adam's advice and planning ahead.

He's also thinking about what happens if he doesn't get a hold of her mother and she doesn't know her daughter has been kidnapped. What if she stays on vacation for weeks? He never planned for a plan B, even though Adam had made a few jokes about it, and tried to bring it up on so many occasions, all the what ifs and things that could go wrong. He had shrugged them all off, so cocky he was when it came to business and running the show. He had been so certain that this was going to work out for them that he never let himself see the alternative. He refused to think past collecting the money, dropping the girl off in the morning, and driving off into the sunset. Stupid. Brandon's just as blinded by money as Adam is about pussy, and he knows it. He's feeling angrier and angrier with himself by the minute. He unlocks the living room door and leaves it open for Adam, expecting him to handle the situation with the girl while Brandon cools himself off.

But Demi sees this open door as her chance to escape. She no longer cares about her role in the situation, the kidnapping, the guys or their guns, or what may happen to her when she tries to break free, she stops thinking clearly and slips into full out panic mode; she just needs out, no one is coming for her and she needs to rescue herself. She doesn't even consider the fact that other doors in the house may be locked, or that realistically, given her life experience, she's not likely to take two full grown men down, even if they weren't armed. She jumps up after Brandon and attempts to chase him out the door, repeating in her mind like a broken record that she needs to save herself.

Adam has been watching the whole thing on pins and needles since Brandon kicked the table towards him, and although he's been ready for some sort of fight from her, he is not expecting this. Her pathetic attempt at an escape almost makes him laugh out loud, but whether she likes it or not, she's going back into that bedroom. He jumps up and he's on her in a split second, grabbing her from behind and half scooping her up in his arms, just like before when he'd brought her in from the van, except he doesn't hold his hand over her mouth this time. Let her squirm and scream if she wants to.

As he starts to carry her towards the room, Demi fights him like crazy, going nuts with the desire to get herself free, and her strength actually takes him by surprise. On top of that, her hot tiny body is kicking and wiggling against him, driving him mad. His clothes on her hide nothing, and she is so determined and flexible, her legs and stomach and soft skin are visible everywhere. His one hand is gripping her thigh, and his other holds her upper arm, pulling her against him. His mind is almost as hard to control as she is as they cross the threshold into the bedroom, and the half chub he's been sporting all morning has turned into a full raging hard on. Forcing her and dominating her like this is doing something to him that he doesn't quite understand.

Brandon hears all of their commotion as he's walking down the hallway, all the moans and groans and shuffles as he leaves, and he can't help but be drawn back in with humored curiosity, some of his sour mood broken. Is Adam really having that much trouble with this girl? He stands and watches them from the doorway with his arms crossed, and if the situation had been any different he probably would have started laughing at his friend's difficulties, struggling to get this 125lbs girl into a closet room; at the moment Adam was pulling her as she clings to the doorway with the one arm she's managed to wiggle free, her upper body half turned towards him in his arms, her knuckles white.

Instead of laughing he just lets out a half ass snort and says "Hey man, looks like you have your hands full with our darling hostage here, but we don't have time for this. So why don't you show her who the boss is here, lock her up in that room and get your fucking ass out to the kitchen with me. Oh, and if all else fails mate, don't forget you have a gun huh?" With that, he gestures to the gun on his own hip and walks out of the living room, leaving the door wide open again, which sends her into over drive at the possibility of her escape being so close.

Adam flushes at the thought of showing her who's boss, and his cock twitches in agreement, until he feels an elbow dig into his side, knocking the wind out of him. She's determined to escape from him and that brings his mind onto more important things for a moment. He doesn't even understand what her urgency is considering he's got a gun attached to his hip that's jamming into her back, and Brandon has just reminded her of that too.

But that gun isn't the only thing that's pressing into her back right now, and he would swear she knows it by the way she's throwing herself against him, wiggling and squirming, trying to break free. This feeling of dominating her is driving him crazy, and he has no intention of grabbing his gun and ending things quickly, even though he could. He had to admit a large part of him is enjoying this, and since he knows she isn't getting away and he's got her either way, there's no harm in letting it play out. What does he have to look forward to after this, Brandon's temper tantrum? He can let himself enjoy their little game for a moment.

Demi can't seem to get herself to calm down and focus. She isn't thinking about their guns, their muscles, or what her actual plan is, she can't think of anything other than getting free of these guys because she knows now that her mother isn't going to come rescue her. She keeps telling herself repeatedly that she just has to escape the guy that's holding her and run past the guy in the hallway, and then she's sure she'll be free. It seems so easy.

A voice in her head keeps trying to break through to her and tell her that she's being ridiculous; they have guns, they're in the middle of nowhere, and for the time being she will be safe, and they won't hurt her, but she just wants this all over with. Her panic attack has taken over her and drowned out her voice of reason.

He's so strong though, he can basically laugh at her attempts to run away. As he pulls her into him again and the gun pokes her hip, the thought of him being armed finally gets through to her. She wonders why he hasn't tried to use it to end this and get what he wants. Instead, he just squeezes her tighter and pulls her in closer, determined to control her by hand. His breathing is getting heavier and closer to her ear, and she is positive that's his cock she can feel pressed up against her ass, since she can feel his gun pushing into her other side. The thought of his gun doesn't stop her though, and she gives it her all in one last attempt to break free before she feels him grab her even tighter and walks into the closet with her, forcing her body onto the cot.

She feels her body thump hard against the mattress and she tries to push herself back up, but suddenly he's got a hard grip on her wrist, and she feels the cuffs slip back onto her left wrist and then onto the bed post. He means business now, and she can't believe that he's about to cuff her up. "Oh my god, no!" She yells at him and tries to kick out and lash at him as he grabs her other wrist, but then her upper body is completely cuffed down. Reality sets in, and she's totally shocked and dismayed by her hysteria and her actions, and she knows she has no one to blame but herself because she lost her cool. She's desperate though, and willing to try anything one last time. She's ready to beg and plead and do whatever it'll take to make him let her go. She's already helpless. She just wants to go home.

"Please," she cries out to him, "you can't leave me handcuffed up like this. I'm sorry! You have to let me go. Please! I promise I will be good!" He gives her an odd look, one she can't read, and then he eyes her up and down. That's when she realizes the shirt she's wearing has hiked up her stomach, and the shorts have done the same thing up her legs. Her stomach, the bottom of her breasts, her thighs and the hint of her panties and her ass cheeks are all visible to him. She feels so exposed. That's what he's staring at. He raises an eyebrow at her and says, "looks good on you," and then exits, shutting and locking the door behind him, leaving Demi in mortified silence.

Demi lays still for a few minutes, forcing herself to calm her breathing and her racing heart. She realizes she isn't going to get anywhere having another panic attack, this one cuffed to an old cot at that. She listens to the younger one walk away, through the living room and hears him shut the living room door behind him. She tries to soothe her mind as well, refusing to imagine all the bad things that could happen next. She's confused and a little scared, but she's trying to accept the scared feeling and then let the scared feeling pass. She doesn't need to add to her anxiety.

She tells herself to focus on the things she does know, or at least the positive sides to the situation. If these guys had wanted to rape her or hurt her, they would have by now. And they certainly wouldn't be putting themselves through all of this aggravation if they could simply fuck it off. They could have done all of that at her house. They aren't going to get any money from her mother if they hurt her either. That's not how kidnappings work. For now, she is safe.

Her mother has probably changed her vacation plans for another week's stay and will likely be in touch again in a few days. Her mother is always doing what she wants without consoling her, without caring about her or what she's doing, she has from the moment her father passed away. Hell, she had been like that before her father died too. Of course, that would make the guys panic and stress about having to re-plan their kidnapping, but they will figure something out and get a hold of her mother. That also means she's likely going to be here longer, if she doesn't rescue herself, and that thought leads her right back to being cuffed to the cot.

From there she keeps replaying what Adam said to her when he walked away, and she keeps seeing the way he had eyed her up and down in his clothes. "Looks good on you." What did he mean by that? And oh, that half smirk. Every time she thinks about it she finds herself blushing, and that knot forms in the pit of her stomach again, that feeling of butterflies. She thinks she knows exactly what he means by that, but she tries to push the thought away. Still, the feeling of his arms around her, his tight muscles, he's strong and clearly has no problem overpowering her and forcing her down, dominating her... Isn't that what she's always wanted, a bad boy with a soft side to dominate her? And damn he's so good looking, and covered in tattoos, he just screams trouble in a good and bad way.

Clearly, she is not doing a great job of controlling her thoughts, and the pit in her stomach begins to spread to an ache between her legs. She throws her head back and sighs, frustrated, and pulls against the restraints while she rubs her thighs together to try and quench the throbbing there. She's kidnapped and she should be scared, she should be crying, she should be anything other than what she's feeling. Yet, here she is restrained, helpless, panties wet, rubbing her thighs together to no avail, aching for her kidnapper to crawl between her legs. It's like one of her bad sexual dreams come to life. What the hell is she going to do? What the hell is wrong with her?

Chapter Six:
Sunday, just after noon

Adam walks down the hallway to the kitchen and finds Brandon pacing the room frantically, impatiently tossing his keys from hand to hand. Adam grabbed the ghost phone on his way through the living room and he tucks it into his pocket for now. The atmosphere in the kitchen is very tense, and Adam starts to ask what the hell is going on, but he's cut off as Brandon tells him to shut up and get in the van. Then without another word he turns and walks out through the kitchen door to the car port. Adam's got no choice now but to follow if he's going to figure out what the hell is going on, but he's hesitant to leave Demi cuffed up like this. Brandon had told him to lock her in the room, but not exactly the way he had done it.

Yes, it'd given him a whole lot of odd pleasure dominating her, and quite a sexual thrill to punish her for acting out, because she had certainly deserved it. Except he hadn't thought much past the guys just talking in the kitchen for a little bit while they came up with a new plan, not leaving the farm house all together. He knows better than to argue with his buddy though, especially when Brandon is in a mood like this, so he keeps his mouth shut and follows him out, making sure the door is locked and secure behind them.

Adam climbs in the passenger side of the van and Brandon drives off almost before he's got the door pulled shut, let alone buckled himself in. The van peels down the driveway so fast that gravel sprays behind them everywhere, and Adam's sure Demi can hear that from inside the house. He wonders what she's thinking, wonders if she thinks they're leaving her there, and then mentally scolds himself for wondering about her at all. Hell, *he* doesn't even know where they are going. He has got to break this hold that she's got over him, it doesn't make any sense, but the thought of her all cuffed up on the cot keeps replaying over and over in his mind, and it's enough to distract his focus from anything.

The guys don't say much for the first few minutes of the drive. Adam stares out the window, not daring to say a word, and feeling like his whole body is made of pins and needles. He realizes that they're heading back into the city. He keeps glancing over at Brandon, who is driving with the steering wheel gripped in a death grip and whose eyes never leave the road. The unknown is killing Adam, and he's trying to work up the nerve to say *anything* when finally, Brandon breaks the silence first and says that they're going to K-Mart.

"K-Mart?" Adam replies in a scoff, totally confused and no longer able to bite his tongue. He feels his anger at everything start to boil over as he talks. "What the fuck are we doing going to K-Mart for? What the hell is going on Brandon? What are we going to do?" Brandon laughs, and then falls silent again, and keeps driving. Adam thinks he may have to lose it before he gets some answers when Brandon finally says, "You sound like the girl. Stop asking so many panicky questions, quit nagging me and get a hold of yourself. I'm trying really hard to keep my shit together as it is."

He pauses for a minute, and then takes a deep breath and continues. "The bitch is screwing us man. Seriously. She isn't coming home from her vacation until Thursday, Thursday, Adam that's 4 days away from now! And apparently that's if she feels up to it. And she doesn't know what hotel she'll be continuing on to, so she'll have to just *reach out again* in a day or two and confirm all of that. And," he grips the steering wheel even tighter as he continues to eye the road, and his knuckles start to turn white. "The *best* part is, apparently, she's lost her cell phone in a pool somewhere, so Demi can't even call her back. Oh, and kisses darling. That's how she ends her voice mail. Prissy bitch. Kisses darling."

It takes Adam a few moments to process all of this. Alright, yeah, can he really blame his friend? Now a lot of his stress and anger is actually justified. They had planned for a few hour kidnapping. Not half of a week, or longer. And he's not even going to mention the fact that he tried to bring up a backup plan only a dozen or more times. He's sure Brandon has reminded himself of that enough already, kicking himself for not listening to Adam in the first place.

If they don't take off today and get all of this dealt with, they both have lives and appearances they will have to keep up, and anything can go wrong in a couple of days. Hell, Brandon has a job, one he's bitched nonstop about having to take time off of for this already, and one he's very grateful to not have to keep going back to. Everything can be suspicious to Brandon. And Adam has some nosy neighbors back in his apartment building. The whole point of this kidnapping was that it was supposed to be a quick and easy job, and for those reasons it wasn't *supposed* to be suspicious. The guys disappearing for the week is going to arouse a lot of questions. And who knows what Demi had planned for this upcoming week that she may be missed from, too?

Tension continues to rise in the van as the guys make the rest of the trip to the store in silence, both lost in their own thoughts about the situation. It feels like the drive takes forever, but eventually Brandon pulls into the K-Mart parking lot and finds them a spot alone near the back. They sit and brainstorm for a few minutes, making a quick game plan for what they are going to need for now. They also don't want to go overboard either, in case they can figure something out for getting this kidnapping over with sooner. They aren't millionaires yet, and the less they have to ditch after, the better.

Brandon's insistent that Demi needs clothes. "She is not sitting around half naked for you to drool over for the next few days and cause you to lose sight of the bigger picture here." Brandon says to him, and for once, Adam agrees without any argument, and without feeling like a scolded teenager either. He knows he has to get that girl off of his mind, and she is far too good looking to be sitting around with her sexy body on display. Besides, he also feels a twinge of jealousy he can't explain at the thought of Brandon drooling over her too, even though he hasn't said too much in that aspect. It's just better that she be covered for both of their sake.

The guys also plan to grab a couple of frozen dinners, some snacks and cheap food for the day or so, and some more liquids, and then decide they will come back to the plan after Brandon's had a chance to make some phone calls and tried to reach Demi's mother again. Adam asks what they are going to do if she really doesn't get a hold of them until Thursday, or what if it takes even longer, but Brandon tells him he won't talk about it. He didn't want to last time and he should have, but that's not going to happen a second time. Done is done. Adam was right the last time, but luck has to be on their side eventually.

They don't spend a long time in the store, both of them are still tense and anxious to get back to the farm house and get things on with. But as the guys walk by the deli, they can smell the chicken roasting, and the sound of their stomachs rumbling causes them to pause for a moment. They had skipped breakfast in their haste this morning, and now it's rolling over lunch. Adam laughs at the sound, and it starts to break up their mood a bit. Brandon suggests that they grab something for a late lunch that doesn't take any cooking, something that they can just throw in the deep fryer or the oven. If they are starving, he can just imagine that Demi is too.

Brandon figures while he throws lunch together quickly, he can also make some phone calls, maybe he can track the girl's mother down elsewhere, see if there have been any reportings of Demi missing, and he's also debating calling in sick to work for tomorrow too, but arguing with himself over whether that's going to affect their cover or not. He doesn't want anything to get anymore screwed up than it already is. He needs some time to do some serious thinking about what to do next, and Adam knows he just needs to let Brandon lead at this point. This is his show, and Adam doesn't want to be responsible for anything going wrong from here on out.

It isn't as easy for the guys to pick out clothes for her as they thought it would be, and their tense mood is totally diminished by the time the two of them are in the ladies' section, browsing and laughing. Between outer clothes, bras, underwear, trying to figure out pant sizes vs shirt sizes and a hundred other odd things they've never thought of, they are so confused, lost and giggling quietly to each other, realizing how little they really "know" about women. Pant sizes range from zeros to 16s and then 21s to 38s, shirts that are a medium in one brand look like a giant in another brands medium, and neither of them have a clue when it comes to bra sizes. They grab her a few smalls and mediums in everything and whatever they think will be sufficient enough to cover her for a few days and then they head for the cash.

Along the way Adam stops and grabs her a stick of deodorant and a toothbrush. Brandon raises an eyebrow at this, wondering again just how well Adam will be able to control himself around this girl, but Adam tells him quietly to put it on her ransom tab. The girl is going to want to feel clean.

The part about the ransom tab gets Brandon laughing, and that gets rid of the last bit of stress that he's been carrying around about Adam. It takes the guys a few more minutes to get through the line and sorted and get everything paid for, then they're packing Brandon's van up with their bags and back on the road. The guys are driving towards the house in about 45 minutes, and the whole trip takes them just over an hour.

On the ride back, Brandon finally feels relaxed and comfortable enough to talk to Adam about the other thing that's bothering him without losing his control or his temper. Now that the guys have shared a few laughs and have a more solid plan, it's easier for Brandon to open up. He tells Adam that he knows he's seen some glances between him and Demi, and regardless of the crazy situation they find themselves in, he *needs* to know that Adam is on the same page. "I refuse to have your sexual frustrations, and a scared sexy girl, ruin millions of dollars and a whole new life for the two of us. In a few days tops you'll be a millionaire, and you can have any girl you want. So please, keep your dick in check for now." Even though his pride is hurt, Adam knows Brandon is right, and he agrees. He knows he does have to keep his feelings under wraps, especially any sexual ones he may have for her. And *especially* if she reciprocates. Besides, he is sick of being told what to do, and hearing the same thing over and over again, both from his buddy and from himself.

They pull in the drive way and kill the engine. It almost feels weird to be back here after they left earlier so tense and in such a hurry. The guys grab their bags from the store and head into the house. It's quiet, there's no screaming or yelling from their captive, and Adam's glad for this. Considering how he left her, he's sure she cannot be happy with him. Brandon takes the bags of food and leaves Adam with the bag of clothes, and Brandon tells him to head down to the living room. "Let her out and give her some clothes and tell her to get dressed and settled. Then when she's ready you can fill her in on the part of the plans that she does need to know." Brandon plans to put lunch together for them, chicken fingers, French fries and some mozzarella sticks, and make some phone calls to inquire about her mother, and then he will be in to join them when the food is cooked.

Demi never even hears the guys come back into the house. She didn't even hear them leave in the first place, for that matter. She has spent the last hour or so lost in a half asleep sexual fantasy, thighs rubbing together, moaning quietly as she pulls against her restraints, soaked in her own juices. It's like she was tied up solely to be teased. Somehow, she let herself get lost once the younger guy left, lost in her feelings of desire, the sexual fantasy naughtiness of the situation, and drowning in her own horny need.

And now; she is feeling utterly mortified when the door opens. Demi jolts up as much as she can, shocked. For a moment it's almost like she forgot where she is, having been left for so long and having given in to the mental side of her sexual cravings, but then she sees Adam, and everything comes flooding back to her, including the fact that she is currently handcuffed to the cot, mostly naked and basically panting and rubbing herself. What a show this has got to be for her kidnapper. She feels all of the blood in her body rush to her face in embarrassment and she throws her head to the side to avoid eye contact with him, completely humiliated. She doesn't even know what to say, and she wouldn't trust herself to open up her mouth right now anyway. Besides, what the hell *could* she possibly have to say for herself?

Adam is totally dumbfounded. He can't believe what he's seeing right now, and any thoughts of controlling himself are long gone out the window; his cock is so hard he feels like he may cum right there in his pants. He isn't sure if he's ever seen such a hot scene in real life. And he can smell her; her scent is strong and musky and calling for him, and he has to stop himself from moaning out loud. He drops the bag in the doorway, and it takes every ounce of willpower he has inside of him not to strip himself naked, climb on top of her and take her right there on the cot, giving her exactly what she seems to be asking for.

Instead, he tells himself that Brandon is in the other room, Brandon will be back in the room any minute, Brandon, Brandon, Brandon. He says his buddy's name a few times in his head like some crazy mantra, focusing on what he has to do. Then he forces himself to walk over to the cot without saying a word, or even attempting to look at her, since she's thrown her face to the side, and he unlocks the handcuffs and turns to walk out. Adam doesn't trust himself to speak any more than to kick at the bag of clothes on the floor with his foot and tell her that they'd picked her up some stuff to wear, and that she's welcome to come out and use the bathroom and freshen up anytime she's ready. With that, he shuts the door to the small bedroom and goes and sits down on the couch, barely breathing, trying to figure out what has just happened, and what the hell he has just seen.

He rubs his face with his hands, feeling so conflicted, fighting so hard with himself to get that scene out of his head, but he's not having much luck. What had he just come back to find? Her hair had been a mess, sprawled out behind her on the cot. Her eyes were wide in shock, it really seemed like somehow, she had just not been expecting him to come back in and find her there; cuffed, horny, helpless and clearly soaking wet. He had been able to smell it, and he swore he still could now. The cot beneath her was probably damp with her juices.

Replaying the scene over and over in his mind is enough to make him crazy. And he has so many questions! Whatever made her act that way? Had it been him and what happened between them before the guys left? Had she enjoyed being dominated and controlled like that? Had she found pleasure in being cuffed up and left helpless, and teased? She just hadn't struck him as such a submissive. His cock twitches at the thought, and he has to stifle a moan. There is no way, he thinks to himself, and yet, that whole fighting, over powering, dominating her scenario has left him with some serious thinking to do. He's tried, but there is simply no way these thoughts are just going to go away now. This girl's mother has *got* to call soon.

Demi turns away from the wall in time to see Adam's back as the door shuts behind him, and hot tears well up in her eyes, threatening to overflow. She is completely mortified, beyond any feeling of embarrassment she's ever felt in her entire life, and man is she ever pissed off with herself for getting carried away like that too. What was she thinking? A little rough play, and not even any actual sexual play with someone should not leave her acting like a horny little vixen. But it just seems like for the first time in her life, she was manhandled by someone who wasn't planning to hurt her, but who she felt touched something inside of her, without even touching her in that way. She feels a weird level of trust with him that she can't quite explain either. Earlier, he could have pulled his gun on her at any moment, or roughed her up, and yet he didn't.

Once she is all alone and she's had a chance to calm herself down a little bit, Demi sits up slowly and rubs the marks on her wrists from where she'd been pulling on the cuffs. She stares at the closed door for a moment, and then lets her gaze fall to the plastic bag on the floor. She remembers what the younger guy had said to her on his way out. They had brought her some clothes? That's something she knows to be grateful for; she's cold and tired of being exposed. She is thankful to have anything that's better to cover up with than the clothes the younger guy had given her to wear and thinking of him causes her stomach to tighten up into knots. She instantly feels horny *and* humiliated all over again. At least having some real clothes on will stop him from looking at me in ways that cause this same reaction, she thinks to herself. Or rather, she hopes it will. She just wants her mother to call and come get her out of here before things get any worse. She hates that she's waiting on her mother for a rescue. She desperately wishes that she could just save herself. It's almost become some sort of mantra for her.

Demi gets up from the bed slowly and picks up the bag of clothes from the floor. She dumps the contents on the bed and examines them. The guys didn't do too bad of a job; they got her jeans and shirts that would most likely fit, and they had done alright with underwear too, although the bras would never work. She will just go without, it won't be the first time in her life. There are perks to being an A cup, and going bra-less is one of them.

She takes a few minutes to get herself dressed, not being in any real hurry to go out into the living room. When she's done getting changed, she notices that they've even got her toiletries at the bottom of the bag. That breaks her mood a little bit and helps her feel a bit more relaxed about the bigger situation; they really wouldn't be planning to hurt her if they wanted her to be comfortable like this. It also helps add to her sense of trust.

The feelings she's experiencing right now though, the humiliation and embarrassment, are of her own doing, if she's going to be honest with herself. They want this over with just as much as she does, because then they'll get their ransom money and be off on a whole new life. At this point she's not sure how many times she's heard the older one say that, and the younger one has mentioned it too; starting over, starting fresh, getting a chance to start a new life, and she almost chuckles before realizing she really is going to have to go back out there and face them... and she sits back down on the bed gently, unsure of herself. *Can* she really go out there?

She hears the creaking of one of the old pull out couches coming from the other room as the younger one adjusts his seating, if the older one hasn't come back too, and she realizes that she doesn't have much choice; if she doesn't go out there, eventually they will just come in here for her. She's not exactly in control of things. And considering all the changes in their plans, and this buildup of sexual tension between her and the younger one, Demi knows the best thing she can do right now is behave and not make any more trouble for them. She is just going to have to suck up her pride and walk out there and be a big girl.

Demi grabs the toiletries from out of the bag, walks over to the door and places her hand on the doorknob. She takes a deep breath and tries to calm her nerves, telling herself in her head that she can do this, that she's strong, she's capable, and she can do anything she puts her mind to, and then she opens the door, keeping her eyes on the floor to avoid eye contact with anyone, and practically runs across the living room and into the washroom. She slams the door behind her, her heart racing, palms so sweaty and shaky she almost drops the deodorant and toothbrush that she's holding. Okay, she scolds herself, that was not cool or calm, and maybe she can't do everything yet, like make eye contact. She may need a few more minutes in here.

Adam watches her skirt across the room, and chuckles to himself as she slams the bathroom door shut behind her. It's almost Deja vu for him from earlier this morning, except she has a lot more clothes on now, and this time her cute little ass isn't hanging out. He doesn't doubt that she's feeling incredibly embarrassed about what he walked in on, but he's still feeling confused too, and horny as hell himself. He has to get these feelings of lust under control, and he finds he's desperately wishing for all of this to just be done and over with already. He wants her gone so they can get their money and forget about this entire ordeal. Although he doubts he'll just *forget* about it. He isn't sure how he is going to make it through the next few minutes with her, and when this is finally done with he will be spending some time satisfying himself with many, many, thoughts of her before he might be able to forget her.

He tidies up the mess from when Brandon kicked out at the coffee table earlier, stacks everything onto the tray and takes it over to the mini fridge. Then he grabs the remote and turns the TV on as he sits back down on the couch. He's flipping channels aimlessly, trying to distract his mind from the scene in the bedroom, but he can't stop it from replaying every time he closes his eyes, blinks, hell it's just repeating itself nonstop. He can't help how hard he gets imagining all of the things he would love to do to her while she was tied up and helpless in that room.

Adam tosses the remote back on the coffee table, frustrated, unable to find anything on TV that keeps his concentration. He glances at the bathroom door that's still closed, wondering if she's ever coming out, and then over to the living room door, wondering if Brandon is ever coming back with lunch to help break the tension he's feeling. He finds himself extremely envious that everyone else seems to have a door to shut themselves up behind, except for him.

When the show that he's stopped on flips to a commercial, he just can't wait anymore; she has been in the washroom a really long time, and he's wondering if she's OK, or if something is wrong. He stands up and walks over to the bathroom door slowly. He doesn't know what to say to her, he just plans to knock and see if she maybe needs anything, play it cool; he isn't about to ask her if she's alright and he doesn't want to end up somehow making things worse or any more awkward then they already are. He can imagine a hundred different scenarios that may be running through her head or that she may be feeling, and he bets there's another hundred more he hasn't thought of yet as well.

Adam takes a deep breath to steady himself and steps up to the door, raising his hand to knock, and at the same time Demi opens up the door and starts to walk out, almost walking into him. She yells out in surprise, totally taken back by finding him standing there. He feels even worse now, and he doesn't have a clue what to say, so they stand there very awkwardly looking at each other while she holds a hand against her chest, and another on the door frame, catching her breath. "I'm sorry," he finally stammers, "I, ugh, I just wanted to see if you were okay. You had been in there a while."

Instantly he wants the floor to open up and swallow him whole, and he wishes he could do this all over again. He feels like an idiot right now; having gone and said the exact things he swore he wasn't going to say to her. Both of them blush in embarrassment at the awkwardness of the situation.

He takes a step to the left to try and let her pass him at the same time she tries to do the same, and then again to the right, and the air between them gets even more tense as they fail at maneuvering and dancing around each other for a moment before figuring it out.

On her way to the couch, Demi takes note of where he had been sitting and chooses to sit on the other couch entirely, putting a big gap of space between them. Adam takes a seat in his old spot and notices she still doesn't even look at him at all; she's staring at the TV, sitting rigidly, and her hands are balled into tight fists on her knees. She hasn't made a peep, hasn't even asked where Brandon is or what they plan to do with her now. He assumes she's probably a little bit humiliated and terrified and isn't going to speak up. He feels the need to break the tension, since neither of them can sit in silence lost in their heads like this, and he has no idea how much longer Brandon is going to be. So much for a quick couple of phone calls, Adam thinks, and he feels his stomach grumble in agreement.

He feels like he's swallowed a bunch of jumping beans as he tries to gather up the nerve to say something to her. His palms are sweaty, and his breathing is shallow. He hates that he's acting so childish right now, like a little boy with a crush. He's a grown man for Christ sake, and he's armed at that. It's time to behave like it. He needs to find some confidence, and his balls.

He takes a deep breath and starts by asking her if she wants a pop or some water or anything else to drink. He hears her mumble something under her breath that sounds like "pop please", and he half smiles to himself, getting up and walking over to the mini fridge and grabbing them a couple of cans of Pepsi. That's a start. He hands her one of the cans and sits back down on the couch, cracking his open and taking a couple of big swallows. Then he begins to fill her in on some of the changes that are taking place, about her mother's change of plans and lost cell phone, though mostly he tells her that his partner is making a few phone calls and lunch, and then he will help fill her in on the rest.

At the mention of lunch his stomach rumbles again and this time hers joins in, but hers makes a noise they can't help but laugh at. Her burst of laughter seems to take her by surprise, and Adam watches in amusement as her hands fly up over her mouth as if to hide the sound. The action makes him laugh, a real true deep laugh, and the sound of it turns Demi's stomach into mush and sets all those butterflies inside of her free. She still isn't completely herself again, and everything about him seems to send her mind into a frenzy and brings her right back to that moment in the bedroom once more. She feels her face flush with heat. Her fingers fiddle with the can in her hands, holding it tightly, playing with the tab and spinning it in circles, desperate for a distraction, for something to do to try and keep herself busy.

Adam watches her fingers curl and twist around the can of pop, her head hung low and her shoulders slumped. He knows she's scared and lost, and he feels pretty torn and conflicted himself. He wants to say something to her, he feels his heart pulling for her, but at the same time he can't get a hold of his emotions or stop the ache for her and doesn't know what he should say. Between replaying that scene in the bedroom over and over again, feeling so desperately horny for her, wanting to pull this poor girl into his arms, and being so angry with himself for not being able to stop this whirlwind inside of him, he feels like his head just might explode. He has to get them talking, about something, anything other than what's going on right now. They both need a *real* distraction. And he has got to lift her spirits somehow, get her mind elsewhere, he has to take control of the situation before things get out of hand. Brandon is right, he needs to get his shit together. Women turn him into jello.

He clears his throat and asks her if she's ever seen the movie that's playing on TV. It's not the smoothest thing he can think of, but it's not specific and he doesn't want to shut her down any more than she already is either. It's also one of the only things he can think of off of the top of his head. The question takes Demi by surprise; she's so consumed by thoughts of what happened earlier, she assumed that he would have been too, and wasn't expecting to be asked anything like that. She takes a minute to refocus and actually pay attention to what's on the screen in front of her, and what he's asked her. She sees they're watching a movie she's seen before, and for some reason this gives her a sense of relief at no longer feeling put on the spot.

Before she opens her mouth though, she realizes how ridiculous that is. Is she really worrying about impressing this guy? She tells herself no, but deep inside her gut tells her yes, which is confusing as hell considering everything that's happening. Demi takes a deep breath, steadies herself and responds that yes, she has seen it, and tells him about her favorite part that happened before they turned it on. They chat for a few minutes about the movie, and regardless of how ridiculous she thinks the reasoning why may be, she can feel her whole body relax and let go of the anxiety she's holding, and the mood in the entire room begins to shift. Now that they have something else to focus on, they don't have to sit there envisioning ripping each other's clothes off.

As the conversation between them carries on and they continue to relax, they start talking more comfortably, and Adam finds himself asking her more personal questions trying to get to know more about her life. He can't help still being drawn to her, and he needs to know more about this woman. He asks her about college and what she is taking or took in the past, and if she likes it. Then he finds himself asking about her work life and her friend life, but he bites his tongue when he thinks to ask about her boyfriend situation. That seems too personal, and he hates to admit that he does *not* want to hear a yes from her.

Demi knows the question is coming though, it almost seems inevitable, and she can't help but feel apprehensive about his questions all together. She doesn't know if he's just genuinely curious and wants to get to know her, or if this may have something to do with the kidnapping and her life. She doesn't know if he's interested in her, or interested in what she's like, because she may be missing for the next few days and they need to know if her absence will be noticed.

For a little bit she starts to let her guard down, it seems like the two of them are connecting on a whole other level; it's like she can almost forget about this crazy situation that they're in together. She needs to make sure she doesn't let her sexual or emotional feelings cloud what's really happening here; these guys have kidnapped her, they are asking her mother for a ransom, and she went and let herself act like a horny bitch in heat in front of the guy who turned her into school girl crush mode. She panicked, didn't do as she was told, was reprimanded for it, and then let herself be humiliated and embarrassed by her sexual appetite. She needs to get a handle on the situation. At least as much as she can.

Adam can almost see her walls go back up, right alongside the tension that starts to build between them again, and he curses himself for having asked her so many personal questions. He knows he went too far when he asks her if she has a lot of girlfriends or goes out to party a lot, and she snaps back, "why do you even care, kidnapper?" There is so much hostility in her voice that it's almost dripping with it, and he wishes he had skipped the last few questions.

He snaps back at her almost as fast without even thinking about what he's about to say, or the repercussions of his words. "Yeah, you know I guess I deserve that, but I'm not the mastermind here, I'm just hired extra muscle, along for the ride." It grows silent between them for a few minutes, as Adam tries to control his anger.

He didn't mean to tell her that Brandon's the one in charge, even though it's obvious. He feels it takes away some of his credibility, and some of the power he has. But once he starts talking, it's like a flood gate opens up inside of him. "I don't even know why I'm here. I guess I didn't really realize exactly what I was getting into. I'm just, I'm fucking stuck right now. I need some real money to get my life back together. And fast." He takes a shaky breath, not realizing he hasn't really been breathing while ranting, and he takes off his hat and runs his hands through his hair. "My buddy brought the idea up to me a few weeks ago, and while it seemed crazy and stupid, it also seemed like it could work, and give me what I'm looking for, a chance to start over and try my hand at a different life, a chance to get away. And once I jumped in a little bit, I got tied in for the long haul, the extra stress, and this!"

He throws his hands up in the air in frustration. "Whatever. I've got nothing to lose anyway, I'm struggling to hold on to one awful job after another, I have no family left who cares, a string of shitty cheating girlfriends behind me and I'm in debt up to my eyeballs. I'm failing my life, and something has to give."

The moment he stops talking, the room falls silent except for the sound of the TV playing in the background. Adam realizes he's been ranting away, and he flushes, feeling very embarrassed. He just finds it so easy to open up and talk to her though, even if he's not sure why. He grabs his can of pop and finishes it off with one long swig, and risks taking a glance at her out of the corner of his eye. He finds her just sitting there, looking back at him, and her expression is unreadable. She hasn't said anything in response, and he feels stupid, and exposed, and suddenly realizes that's probably a lot like she has been feeling since he returned from K-mart and found her in the bedroom. Exposed. He lets out a nervous laugh and says, "I guess it's my turn to get personal and be embarrassed," and he's surprised and a bit relieved when she laughs in return, joining in with him on his awkward joke, instead of shutting down again. Silence falls between them once more, but this time it's a little less stressful, and they both fall back into the movie as a distraction, although their thoughts are elsewhere.

Demi can't help but admire her kidnapper; his open honesty shows that he has a heart and a soft spot inside even if he can't admit that or doesn't see it himself. He didn't have to be this nice to her. He has obviously led a hard life, and she can sympathize with him there; she knows all about a hard life. It can make you cold, make you lose your trust in others, it can make you shut out all the good and love in your life for fear of being hurt, and with that comes bad decisions, like bad relationships, failed jobs, and wrong life choices, like kidnapping.

She finds herself thinking, "Once again, thank you therapy." She is grateful all of that time on a shrink's couch has given her something to work with here. She catches herself staring at his muscular arms, remembering how they felt wrapped around her earlier, holding her tightly, so sure of himself and so in control of her and what happened to her. She finds herself thinking about what his life would have been like before all this, what he's really like outside of here, and what he'll do with the money when this is all done and over with.

Try as she might, all she finds herself picturing is him on a hot sunny beach somewhere, wearing nothing but swim trunks, with a set of abs to match those arm muscles and more tattoos than she can currently see right now. The thought of him half naked at the beach makes her stomach clench together, and her breathing speed up a notch, and brings her thoughts right back full circle to the bedroom again. She blushes from head to toe and feels herself growing embarrassed. Will she ever be able to let that go?

Adam may be looking at the TV, but his real focus is on her, absorbing everything that he can, while lost in a whirlwind of confusion. He is watching closely from the corner of his eye, so taken by her, and he notices when she starts breathing heavier and starts to flush again; her t-shirt clinging tighter to her chest, her nipples pushing back against the material. Oh God, he thinks to himself, she isn't wearing a bra. He can't help but feel his cock harden again as the images of her cuffed up and horny on that cot fly through his mind on repeat now. Just like her, he can't seem to let that scene go. It was too hot, too unexpected, too left field considering everything that was going on at the time, and now he's the one starting to flush and breathe hard, lost in thought.

They can feel the sexual tension crawling back into the room, and the silence between them is no longer as comfortable as it was only a few moments ago. She's fidgeting constantly and avoiding looking his way. Adam is determined not to let this happen again, or at this rate Brandon is going to come in with lunch and not only be able to smell sex in the air but be able to cut the sexual tension in here with a knife as well. Thinking of Brandon, he wonders what's taking him so long. He takes a deep breath and can smell chicken and assumes it should only be a few more minutes before they are no longer alone together. He's oddly grateful for that, he doesn't know how much more of this he can take. Besides, this whole thing could be over with soon.

Adam shakes his head to clear his thoughts and stands up and stretches. He's feeling antsy and needing to do something. He wishes for some fresh air and a change of pace, but he'll take a walk across the living room and back, that's as good as it's going to get right now. He can feel Demi's eyes staring into the back of his head, but he refuses to turn and look at her. He walks over to the fridge and thinks about calling back to her over his shoulder instead, asking her if she would like another drink. He can't look at her until he feels he's more in control of himself.

Every time he tries to get himself together and feels like he's over it, and her, and all of her sexiness, she will give him a look (whether she even means to or not), or the smell of her will get to him, or any one of so many thoughts of her now will catch him off guard and send him right back. He can't understand why she is getting under his skin like this; is it just a lack of recent sexual activity? Is it a lack of sleep? Is it because she is just so god damn sexy? Was it seeing her cuffed up and helpless, and loving it, a sight he has never seen a girl in before? Man, it had been something straight out of a porno movie, or a wild fantasy, something he's always wanted from a woman. This whole thing makes him feel like a teenager.

Or, is it because for some reason, while not really knowing how to explain it even to himself, he feels a deep connection with her? Something he just can't put his finger on. He needs some time to figure out what he's feeling, and it isn't helping to be so close to her, being alone with her, with nothing to distract them from each other while they are locked up alone together in this room, in the same space, breathing the same air. He tells himself it won't be for much longer.

He stands in front of the fridge for a bit, gathering his thoughts, trying to calm himself. He takes a deep breath and forces his hands to stop shaking by running them through his hair again, giving himself something to do, tossing his hat over in the corner with his jacket for now. For a few minutes, he needs to push all sexual thoughts of her out of his mind. He needs to take control just until Brandon gets back, and then he can regroup again. He just wants to get through the next few days, get his money, and get out.

Demi watches as he almost drags himself to the bar fridge, clearly deep in his thoughts. It's not lost on her that something is up with him. She can see his shoulders slump and she's torn, she doesn't know what got him upset or what she's done but she knows she may have something to do with his confused attitude. She wishes she could go back in time and erase that entire bedroom scene. She's still baffled with herself, and it cannot be helping her kidnapper here.

When he takes a few minutes longer at the fridge than he needs to, standing there with the door open lost in thought, Demi gets up slowly, thinking maybe she will walk over and ask him what's wrong, or something, because his silence and his turned back are getting to her. She's only a foot away from him though when he gets up and turns around, leaving the fridge wide open, and he's startled to find her so close to him, just as startled and taken aback as she is by his sudden change in posture.

He was finally about to ask her what she wanted to drink, and they can both feel a cool breeze along their legs from the open fridge door as they just stand there. Demi is speechless; being this close to him, smelling him, almost touching him, she's forgotten why she stood up in the first place, and she's slowing losing any control she had over herself. Adam almost cries out loud when he turns around and finds her *right there* in front of him. She's so close their arms are almost touching. What the hell was she doing behind him? He feels like he can't breathe, and suddenly that breeze from the fridge door means nothing, the temperature in the room seems like it just shot up fifteen degrees.

Neither of them say a word, they just look at each other, confused and uncertain, lost in each other's eyes. She is breathing heavily, and he is close enough to her that he can see the vein in her neck pulse as her heart races, he can see her bottom lip sticking out at a slight pout, begging to be sucked on, he can see her chest rise and fall with each shaky breath. His cock is pulsing in his jeans, almost crying out for her, and he doesn't think he's been this hard over someone since his virgin days. His boxers feel stiff with pre-cum. Adam loses all control of himself and his actions, lost in the moment. He is drowning in her big brown eyes, her beautiful face, her tight body, his sexual attraction to her. And he feels himself giving in to everything he's been craving and desiring.

Without even thinking about what he's actually doing, he reaches out with his free hand and grabs her lightly around the neck, pulling her into him, anxious for her. Her eyes close automatically, and her breath catches in her throat for a moment in anticipation of what's to come. She moans, instantly feeling like she's turning to putty in his hands. His thumb caresses her neck lightly, and he can feel her tremble and vibrate under his touch. Her entire body is electrified, and she lets out another soft whimper as she feels her stomach knot up and her panties grow wet with longing. She hasn't realized just how badly she wants this man, needs this man, craves this man, a man whose name she doesn't even know, until he leans in and presses his mouth against hers.

The feeling of her soft wet lips breaks the last thread of self-control that Adam has left. He lets out a small moan himself and pushes against her, grinding his hips and his cock into her, pulling her body closer to him. He drives his tongue into her mouth, needy, urgent, carnal, wanting all of her. Her whole body trembles against him. It only lasts for a few moments, but for the two of them it's an eternity, locked in their deep wet, taboo kiss.

Chapter Seven:
Sunday, sometime before 2

There's a bang from somewhere down the hallway, and the sound jolts them both back to reality, quickly making them realize what's going on, and reminding them that they are not alone. Adam pulls away from her in such a haste, terrified to be caught, acting like a young kid about to be busted by his parents. He pushes past Demi so fast she almost stumbles, but then catches herself, in shock and totally taken aback by the entire thing.

The mini fridge is still wide open, and she feels the cool draft touch her legs again as the heat between them fades and she watches him retreat to the couch. He doesn't dare to look at her, and she wouldn't even know what to say or do if he did. Demi's in complete disbelief that any of this just happened; but her throat is still tender from his touch, she can feel the firm pressure of his lips against hers, warm and wet, and her panties are soaked, her pussy practically calling for him.

She can't seem to understand her bodies reactions and why she's turned on so badly. Why is she acting like some kind of slut right now? Is it because being tied up and roughed around by someone so damn sexy, someone she can trust, brings out something deep inside of her? Is it because this boarder-lines on some sort of fantasy, one where she knows nothing bad will actually happen to her, like consensual in-consent? Isn't that what she's been craving and lacking her whole adult life anyway? A healthy, sexually active relationship in which to explore herself in. So, can she really blame herself? But, why him, her kidnapper, why this situation? Why now? Is this some sort of cruel life joke? Why couldn't she have met someone like him at a Starbucks, or tinder, anywhere normal?

Her head is pounding from all the questions and thoughts that are flying around in there. She knows a full-blown headache is only moments away from creeping up behind her eyebrows; she hasn't had a bad stress migraine in a long time, but they are awful, and she doesn't need one now. She has got to settle herself down. Especially before the older one comes back into the room. She grabs a can of pop from the fridge and finally shuts it, not bothering to grab anything for the younger one, and sits back down on the opposite couch, staring at the TV.

Adam watches her out of the corner of his eye, not daring to speak to her, or make a sound. She's clearly having some sort of mental discussion with herself, and he isn't about to interrupt her. He has his own battles to deal with, and he sits back on the couch in silence, lost in his thoughts. Besides, he isn't about to have a conversation with her about all of this when Brandon could come in at any moment. And what would he say anyway?

He still can't believe he grabbed her and kissed her like that. He doesn't understand why he did it, and doesn't quite regret it, but he can't stop thinking about it either, and that's bad. He's totally blown away and pissed off with himself at his lack of self-control, he's confused and anxious and he just wants to leave; he wants to grab his keys and his small bag of stuff and call it quits, lock her in the living room and walk out right past Brandon in the kitchen, give him the peace sign, see ya later man, keep my share of the money, and just go.

But he knows better than that, he's in this too deep now, and it's not like this was unexpected anyway; Brandon has been telling him nonstop to quit looking at her like that, to stop thinking the thoughts he's thinking, to let it go, to put his dick away, and he knew better than this himself! So, isn't this exactly what he deserves? He mentally scolds himself, thinking that he always screws his life up because of women, and here he's gone and done it again. The biggest problem is, he just can't figure out why he's so drawn to this girl in the first place, what is it about her? If he's honest with himself, he would almost give it all up to take her right here, pin her and cuff her to the couch, and bury his cock deep inside of her. All of this sexual craziness would be over with, and right now it seems worth it.

There's another noise as Brandon *finally* comes back down the hallway with food, and they're both dragged out of their thoughts and snapped back into reality. Demi feels herself blush from head to toe in utter embarrassment, it's almost as if she's been up to something naughty and is about to be busted. It dawns on her that the older guy would likely have had no idea about the scene his friend walked in on, or the kiss, or anything. He has been out in the other room the entire time.

Adam's having very similar thoughts fly through his head; it's not like it's entirely his fault, and it's not like Brandon even knows what Adam walked in on, or that they've kissed, but he still feels extremely guilty about it all and he knows it shows all over his face. He has told himself a thousand times over that he was *not* going to let his stupid dick get the best of him, but now he's gone and done just that. Well, maybe not quite with his dick, but he always does though, one way or another, and Brandon is going to see it, and know it, and somehow everything will be jeopardized because of it. Stupid.

Brandon's whistling to himself as he comes into the living room. It may have taken him a bit longer than he had expected to make his phone calls, but he's feeling a lot more confident about the situation now and his mood has lifted incredibly. He turns and locks the door behind him, and instantly seems to be hit by the wall of tension in the room. These two kids are ridiculous, he thinks to himself, can't leave them alone for a minute. He's hoping the change of news will break it up a bit. Before (and after) his phone calls, he'd been trying really hard to bring his mood back around so he's more mellowed out and doesn't lose his shit, and he isn't going to let these two and their teenage-like hormones make it worse.

He assumes Adam did something dumb, it's Adam, and that's what Adam does. Brandon guesses he probably made a pass at the poor girl and she likely shot him down because, well, that's pretty obvious too. He wonders if she slapped him or hit him, and almost wishes that he'd been in the room for that. He chuckles to himself, raises the tray full of food at the pair of them and then winks at Demi and says "See, I am a man of many talents, not just a handsome kidnapper of pretty ladies by night."

Demi isn't sure whether to laugh or to be offended at his remark, and so she doesn't say anything while she watches him set the tray down on the coffee table by the TV, but his comment clearly breaks up the tension for Adam, who lets out a great big laugh, that deep stomach laugh she's already being drawn to so much. Despite the knot in her stomach and her still wet panties, she feels the tension in the room diminish significantly in that moment of relaxation. Demi lets herself loosen up a touch and laughs with him, but the moment is lost as soon as they lock eyes and her stomach tightens even more. Would this never end? She tears her eyes away and looks at the food and then at the other guy, determined to keep herself focused now.

Brandon chuckles and gestures to the food, it's a little ways past lunch now and been quite some time since they've ate anything. He takes her frustration as hunger, and he doesn't want to see the girl starving; that wouldn't look good on them either, dropping her off haggard and skin and bones. He waits until Demi and Adam have begun to eat, and then he makes himself a plate, grabbing a few chicken fingers and picking away. He thinks he's been doing a good job of keeping up a front, but he is secretly stressing inside and doesn't have much of an appetite.

Brandon can feel Adam's eyes baring into him, and the girl's desperation beside him, and the growing tension between them all. At least the girl seems to have a great appetite, she is scarfing down food right now. Brandon only manages to get one whole chicken finger into him though before Adam can't contain himself anymore and asks him what the new plans are. The anxiety and tension are clearly killing his partner, and here he had thought Demi would be the first to crack, eager to go home. He licks his fingers and then holds one up in a gesture to tell them to give him a minute. He gets up and grabs a beer from the mini fridge, cracks it and sits back down again, thinking about where to start.

"Well, I did some snooping around," and then he winks at Demi, "because that's another one of my specialties. I am pretty sure I have found out which hotel your mother is staying at, but I haven't got a for sure confirmation on that yet, so I haven't made contact. Once I know that's where she's staying, I need you to call and leave a message for her stating that she needs to call this ghost number with some serious news. I want your voice on the phone, so she knows this is real. Once she calls, I will let her know about the kidnapping and all of the money transfer details, and then we can go from there. But we sort of have to plan for Thursday at this point, just in case."

He pauses for a moment, and then he gives Adam a nod. "You were right from the beginning, we have to start planning for the what ifs now." Then he turns his attention back to Demi. "Sucks that she would leave you hanging without much notice or contact like that though. You would have drove all the way to the airport this morning for nothing. Not much of a motherly thing to do." He pauses for a moment to let the news sink in for them, and then realizing he left it on such a downer note, says "But, seems like we saved you a wasted trip! And we'll make your time here fun! Board games and movies and bad jokes!" And laughs at his attempt at bad humor to try and keep the mood, and himself, up.

The mood in the room doesn't stay happy though. In the silence that follows, Demi can feel misery seeping its way into her brain, shutting her down and extinguishing any lingering sexual feelings she may have had for the guy sitting across from her, and that miserable feeling spreads out into the room. The guys turn their attention to the TV in the silence. She's stuck here even longer now because her mother doesn't really love her, doesn't care about her, and hasn't even bothered to pretend to since her father died. If she did, she would have been at the airport when she said she was going to be, coming home to her daughter who was asked to pick her up, or she would have been in contact long before she made more plans like this, and Demi wouldn't have necessarily been home alone in bed waiting to pick her mother up early. She feels like she's all on her own now and needs to be able to rescue herself.

With her thoughts running wild, Demi's barely able to stifle a sob. The guys cast a glance her way, wondering if she's going to be alright. She can't help herself, her thoughts and emotions are all over the place, and when she opens her mouth, a flood gate opens with it and all the words inside come pouring out. "She left that message because she's a shit mother who doesn't love me and doesn't care about what happens to me. She's not even going to care that I've been kidnapped, other than worry about what it'll do to her reputation if anyone ever finds out about this. She's going to pay your money and not even ask how I am. Hell, she'd probably pay you the money to keep me, or kill me. Gone from her life just like my father. Simple and easy." At that, she stifles another sob and gets up and runs to the bathroom, slamming the door behind her. She feels unbelievably embarrassed, and so very sad, and she needs a few minutes to let herself feel these emotions before she regains herself from the entirety of the last 15 hours or so and gets her composure together and regroups. She needs to let things out or she will never get through to Thursday like this.

The guys watch her leave in silence, neither attempting to stop her. They both know she is going to need a bit of time to get herself together, and they aren't eager to open that can of worms right now, or before she's ready. Brandon especially is not about to let Adam get involved in her drama or her emotions, and he has no problem expressing that once more. "Listen man, I will say it again, and again, and however many more times I need to until you get it. You have a thing for troubled fish. Fucked up girls that need help, who you can't save and shouldn't be involved with or be trying to help save in the first place, and *that's* why your life is always a mess." Adam goes to say something, almost feeling like he's being judged, but Brandon cuts him off and continues.

"Now I'm not perfect and I'm not saying I am, hell, I'm just as blinded by money sometimes as you are by pussy. I make a lot of bad choices myself in that regard, just look at what we're doing for a quick buck! But right now, with this girl in this situation, I know that's bad news for all of us, and it's going to screw this whole thing up. Yeah, it's a sad story, and I'm sure you feel bad for her, but you're not the only one feeling for her. I have a tiny heart too you know. And yes, she's super-hot, and I'm sure she'd be a wonderful lay. But I won't let your dick, or mine, come between us and a new life. Because hey, let's face it, under other circumstances I'd totally see if she'd go out with me too. So, let it go man. Just let her be and focus on the job at hand."

As much as Adam knows his friend is right, he's getting tired of hearing it, especially since he keeps repeating the same things to himself too. Though he also finds he can't help but feel another twinge of jealousy at what Brandon said about Demi being fine and nice to look at, and how he'd like a chance to be with her too. He pictures that scene in the bedroom again, and the kiss that they shared, and god dammit! It's in that moment of feeling irritated, and sexually frustrated again so quickly, that he knows he's done for by her, no matter what he tries to do or tell himself.

He gives Brandon a shrug and tells him he knows he's right, and then goes back to nursing his beer and watching the TV, feeling annoyed. There isn't much Brandon can say back to that and he knows it; he's not an idiot, he's aware Adam is full of it, but he also isn't about to start a fight with him about it right now either; he's just got to keep an eye on the situation and do his best to make sure nothing stops them from pulling this off without a hitch and getting away with some big moola.

He's been checking his personal phone religiously, pulling it out of his pocket every 30 seconds or so waiting for a reply from someone, and it isn't long before he gets one.

"Found her!" He says to Adam, looking up from his phone with relief all over his face.

Demi splashes some cold water on her hot skin and takes a few deep, calming breaths. These confusing and conflicting emotions she's experiencing need to go away. She has to get a hold of herself, she's a good part of the reason things are spiraling out of control here, and if she doesn't chill out she's only going to end up making things worse for herself. It's time to acknowledge that she may still have some issues to deal with, emotionally and sexually, and that this whole kidnapping thing might just be bringing them out. And besides, didn't her therapist say a situation similar to this is a normal fantasy for so many women, and hadn't it been one of her own for a long time? Though realistically, in a fantasy a woman has control of the situation and isn't hurt; it's hot, captivating, naughty, thrilling, and all your dreams come true right? But then you can wake up after, or open your eyes, and it's all over.

This whole kidnapping boarder-lines almost exactly on that whole taboo fantasy thing, so can she really blame herself for the way she's been acting? Especially when she considers everything that's been going on in her life prior to this, with therapy opening up so many questions inside of her, and all of her sexual frustration from lack of exploration and trusting partners to have fun with? This thought makes her laugh to herself. And because of this, can she really blame herself for letting her guard down so easily? Because when her guard goes down, her emotions go haywire, and that's what's gotten her here, crying in the bathroom in the first place.

She takes another deep breath, looks at her reflection in the mirror and in her head, she says she deserves to be proud of herself. She's in a bad situation, and yet she has done what her therapist is always telling her to do. Take some time, assess the *whole* situation, and calm herself down before she snaps or has some sort of emotional break down. She no longer feels so angry with herself and she decides she's going to take control of things as much as she can. What happened, happened. But going forward, no more putting herself out there to him in anyway. She can tell by how he lets his buddy take the lead, she feels it's safe to assume he isn't out there talking about what he saw, or what had happened between the two of them. It can be put to rest for now, the younger guy isn't about to upset the balance that's holding this together.

She takes one last deep, calming breath and she's just about ready to open the door and come out of the bathroom when there's a knock on it, startling her. Her heart flutters for a moment, hoping it's the younger one, but she pushes the thought aside; she isn't putting herself out there anymore, remember? Why should it matter? Then she forces herself to open the door, only to be greeted by the older guy with that big stupid handsome smile on his face. "Are you doing OK? I found out which hotel your mom is staying at for sure. Are you ready to come out and make that phone call now sweetheart?" She is so taken back by his ridiculous comedy act for a second time that this time she actually laughs despite how she's feeling, and some more of the tension she has leaves her. "You're such a jerk," she replies with a smile, "I don't understand how you can keep up with such a goofy personality. Fine, let's go do this." "That a girl!" He replies with a wink and follows her back to the couch.

Adam watches the exchange between them at the bathroom door with a little touch of envy and tries to shake it off as she follows Brandon back to the couch and sits down beside him. Adam can't keep his eyes off of her, he can't help himself. He's really admiring her courage and her spirit right now. In all honesty, she could tell them both to go fuck themselves, they could have to threaten her with the guns, he or Brandon may even have to make the phone call, hell, she hadn't even had to give them the idea of calling into her cell phone answering machine in the first place, but she's actually being cooperative and helpful and isn't acting like a terrified little girl. She isn't screaming, causing a scene, freaking out or throwing a fit (other than that one emotional outburst), and she isn't being unnecessarily bitchy to them.

And all of that is besides the fact that Demi clearly has some serious issues with her mother outside of this kidnapping, and certainly doesn't seem eager to chat with her or ask for her help. It's killing him that throughout all of this he's sitting here caring about her and her situation, and it's eating him apart that he can't get that scene out of his head, or stop tasting her on his lips and tongue. And he can't stop the throb in his pants and the ache to just bury his cock inside of her. He feels like his head is going to explode. He forces his attention on Brandon and the job at hand; if she can keep herself together considering it's her that this is all happening to, the least he can do is try to do the same.

Brandon scoots closer to Demi on the couch and picks up the ghost phone from the table. He then pulls a small scrap piece of paper from his pocket that has the number of the hotel on it and holds it between his fingers. "This is the number for the hotel your mother is staying at. You're going to call the hotel and get the switch board," he says to her, "and I want you to tell them that you're trying to track down your mum for a family emergency. If you can't be redirected to her room to leave a message, you're going to ask to leave one at the front desk for her, but the message will be the same. You with me so far?" She gives him a nod, eyes on the cell phone in his hand. It's as if he can see the wheels turning in her head, watching a plan form.

"I am going to be sitting right here beside you, with my hand on the phone if I have to, and my other hand on my gun. Don't forget I have that. I need to be able to trust you. The moment a word comes out of your mouth that sounds like something I haven't told you to say, I will snatch this phone away from you, and there will be consequences. Big ones. Are you with me on that too?" Demi nods again, but she can't help letting a smart-ass remark of her own slip out before she bites her tongue. "But my memory sucks, so make it short, or there will be a lot of consequences."

So much for trying to keep his attention focused on the job at hand. Adam snorts out a laugh, drawn back to her again and the cheeky look on her face. And he feels his cock twitch at the word "consequences." Brandon can't help but chuckle either. This girl has a lot of spirit, he thinks to himself. "Alright, fine, smarty pants." Brandon replies to her, continuing on with what needs to be done. "Within reason, you will say what I am telling you to say now. I won't pull my gun out unless you make me. Just say that there has been a family emergency. You can leave the family part out if you get redirected to her answering machine, I've done my homework and I know it's just the two of you, and you don't need to sound like an awkward robot with a gun to your head. Tell them, or the machine, that you can be reached at this number." He flips the piece of paper over and the other side has the number of the ghost phone on it. "Leave the number clearly, repeat that it's an emergency, and then hang up. And, if you happen to get a hold of her, you can simply hand me the phone, and I will take it from there, and then maybe this will all be over with. That's it. Is that clear and simple? Do you think you can remember all of that?" She sits quietly for a few moments and thinks it over, running it through her head, then nods. This isn't the time for anything crazy and she knows it, even though she has a great rebuttal for that last comment too.

Brandon types in the number for the hotel and hands her the phone, then sits back and watches her carefully, paying close attention to everything she does. She hits send and places the cell phone to her ear. Adam would be a fool to pretend he isn't interested in what's happening, he's gone from watching out of the corner of his eye to full out turning in his spot towards them, staring intently. He's really admiring her strength right now, and almost wants to laugh at the irony; she clearly hates her mother a lot, and hates having to make this phone call, yet here she is about to ruin her mother's extra vacation.

All at once, he realizes that there's a possibility her mother could be at the hotel right now, just like Brandon said. This might all be over soon, Demi's mother could wire them some money, hop on a plane, whatever it takes, and then the guys will be rich and leaving this all behind. And isn't that what he wants? Then why does the thought that she may already be leaving give him a pit of sadness in his stomach? Adam forces himself to clear these thoughts away. Obviously, her leaving now would be a much better solution than him being stuck here with her until Thursday, with him being the loose cannon that he is.

Demi takes a deep breath and waits for the phone to ring. It does, just once, and then right before the second ring it's answered by a sweet woman receptionist stating the name of the hotel and asking if she can help. A voice inside Demi's head screams out "YES! Yes, you can help me! I've been kidnapped, please just call the police! Rescue me without involving my mother!" But instead, she takes another deep breath and tells the clerk that her name is Demi Romaro and there has been a family emergency. As far as she knows, her mother has checked into this hotel. She doesn't know the room number, but she needs to get a hold of her ASAP, it's *super* important. Either being transferred through to her room or leaving a message at the desk is fine, as long as her mother gets it.

She feels the guys eyes on her intently, waiting for some kind of response, and she almost laughs. They probably should have thought about having her put this call on speaker phone if they needed to know every word that's being said, she thinks to herself, but she's not about to do their job for them. She listens as the clerk tells her that she's really sorry she can't put her through to a hotel guests room, but she will gladly take a message and make sure it gets received ASAP. Demi can't explain the weird sense of relief she feels at knowing she won't actually have to speak to her mother right now. She waits for the clerk to grab a piece of paper and a pen, and then she repeats and spells her name, her mother's name, that it's a serious family emergency, and that her mother is to call this number ASAP. Then she recites the number from the paper Brandon is holding in front of her face, thanks the clerk, and hands the phone back to Brandon without bothering to turn it off. He can do the rest.

Brandon hangs the phone up and puts it back onto the coffee table. "Well, that's that." he says, mostly for something to say. He had been really hoping that they would transfer Demi to her mother's room, and then she'd be on the other side of the phone. He was sure this was all about to be over with, and now nothing is going to plan. He can almost feel the tension begin to creep back into the room.

"Well, that's that is right," Demi speaks up, repeating him, taking the guys by surprise, "and now we wait, and wait, back to the waiting game again; while realistically my mother is out having an extended fun vacation on the beach somewhere boozing it up and not giving a shit about me, I'm being held captive by two handsome thugs at gun point, thugs who feed me good food and let me watch bad TV." With that she leans forward to the tray on the coffee table and begins to prep her plate full of food again and eat, not looking at the guys, keeping her eyes on the TV while she stuffs her face.

Brandon lets out a chuckle at her outburst of anger and emotion, she seems to be full of surprises he isn't expecting, and he gets up to go to the mini fridge to grab them all a beer. It's early but he feels they could all use one to help ease the mood. He hands one to Demi and tells her he needs to keep up with the whole feeding her well and taking care of her thing she boasted about, and she smiles back at him and takes the beer. He's also thinking that she could use one to relax a little.

She likes this older guy, he's really good at making her feel comfortable despite the temper she knows is just floating below the surface, and she starts to feel like she can probably get through the next few days just fine as long as he stays in control and she doesn't need to be alone with the one that makes her feel funny all over. They did not bring her enough changes of panties for 4 days with how wet he makes her.

While Brandon and Demi seem to be enjoying themselves chatting and acting much more relaxed together now, Adam's insides are in turmoil. He's so confused about his feelings and his lack of control; he knows that he's been stupid in the past before with women, but this girl is tearing him apart. She has depths he hasn't expected, she has spunk, she has spirit, she certainly has sexual appetite and a naughty side to her, and of course, she seems to be damaged and full of baggage. She's practically everything he's ever wanted in a woman, and all of the things that he doesn't want, too.

Every time he tries to get a hold of himself and stop thinking about her like that, she's all he can think about. He can't seem to get a handle on things. And that scene from the bedroom is going to be etched in his mind forever. He'll be jerking off to it in his old age, wishing he'd been able to just pin her down and take her. He's been so hard all afternoon it's almost uncomfortable at this point. Oh, what he wouldn't give to take his release with her, anywhere but here.

He finds himself starting to daydream about just that, meeting her somewhere else, and being able to actually explore these feelings he has for her, sexually and emotionally. Maybe running into her in a park somewhere, spending time with her at the beach, taking a long road trip with her, her wearing a short skirt, hair flying in the wind, legs spread, his hand making its way up her soft thigh. Would she be wearing underwear?

Her laughing at something Brandon's said brings him back from his day dream. What is he doing day dreaming about her like this anyway? He has a job to do. The whole reason he's even met her is because he's kidnapped her. Truth be told, Adam's a broke ass loser with no money who doesn't have a damn thing going for him anyway. Once this is all over with and he HAS money, and an opportunity to do something with his life, why would she want anything to do with him then, her kidnapper? He's being an idiot. Here he is daydreaming about being with her, and living a life with money, with her, when they kidnapped her in order to let her *go* for money. They'd taken her against her will in the middle of the night, scared her, humiliated her, and sexually embarrassed her (although that one was totally on her) and here he is thinking about a whole other scenario and a life with her. Dumb. Besides, it goes against *all* the preaching he's getting from Brandon, and from himself.

He glances up from his beer, no longer lost in his thoughts, and realizes that Demi and Brandon are both staring at him. He flushes in embarrassment. "Did I miss something," he asks, caught off guard and it comes out a bit gruffer sounding than he means it to. "No man," Brandon replies, giving him an odd look that Adam can't quite read. "Can you pass me the TV remote though? I'm going to try to find us a movie to watch." Adam reaches over to the remote that's sitting on the couch beside him and hands it to Brandon, seeing that the movie they had been watching has already ended, credits and all. No wonder they were looking at him funny. He'd been checked out in his head for a while. He refuses to get lost in thought like that again, he swears to himself, even if he has to sit here and pinch himself while focusing on every word on the TV and that Brandon and Demi say. Get your shit together, he scolds himself.

Brandon finds a comedy movie on TV, thinking that they could all use a little bit of comic relief. Laughter is the best medicine after all. He tries to get as comfortable as he can on the couch, even though it feels like he's got ants in his pants. He keeps looking at the phone on the table like it's a ticking time bomb, just waiting for it to ring. And he's not alone in that feeling.

Demi can't help risking glances at the younger one out of the corner of her eye as the movie plays. He looks so irritated and pissed off right now, troubled, confused, and while she can't exactly blame him, she can't stop thinking and wondering to herself, what about that kiss? She can't figure out what happened earlier, they have some weird chemistry she doesn't understand, and she wants to know how he feels about the whole thing. She's dying to know what caused him to grab her and kiss her, and if that was why he seems so off now. Clearly, he would regret something like that and wish this whole thing was over with. Right? She figures that's what was getting to him now, and he's probably just waiting for all of this to be over with. She feels herself sigh, she can't help it. Why would he want to be around her any longer than he needs to be? Because of one kiss?

Chapter Eight:
Sunday, closer to dinner

As time continues to pass and the second movie begins to reach its climax, the mood in the room starts to tense up again. The seconds feel as if they're passing like minutes, and minutes drag by like hours. They all begin to grow extremely restless and fidgety. No one is talking at all, not even small talk, and when the movie finally ends, and the credits are rolling Brandon can't take it any longer; he jumps up and begins collecting and stacking all of the dishes that have been sitting since lunch time. "I've got to make some more phone calls," Brandon says, "this sitting around and waiting is killing me. Maybe I can see if there's a way I can make things happen faster, and regardless I need to start making a better plan. And to make us some more coffee. And I need to figure out dinner later, and a better food plan until Thursday, just in case. If I need you Adam, I'll holler for you. You two just sit tight for a bit and don't do anything stupid."

He looks at Adam specifically and then winks at Demi, and she can't help but feel herself blush, desperately hoping that neither of them noticed. What the hell is wrong with her? "And obviously if you need me, you have the keys to get out. And a gun, if things get crazy." Brandon finishes, looking back at Demi once more before taking all the dishes and empties on the tray as well as the extra tray from on the mini fridge and leaving the living room, locking up behind him.

The moment he shuts the door, the tension in the living room grows again tenfold. Neither Demi nor Adam want to risk talking to each other, or even looking at each other, they keep their eyes glued on the TV, lost in their own thoughts. They aren't thrilled to be alone together again. They are both replaying that kiss over and over, back to back with the scene from the bedroom. And they're both over flowing with so many questions. Demi's stomach is in knots. She's so anxious she feels sick with the unknown. Why he had kissed her at all? He'd had plenty of opportunity to take advantage of her if sex or rape was what he was after, so did that mean he likes her then? That he kissed her simply because he wanted to? That's absurd, isn't it? She's so confused. He can't possibly like her. He certainly hasn't been acting like he likes her, but then again, what's he really supposed to do, or say? Just cuddle up to her, and ask her for a date when all of this is over? Or while she's kidnapped? This whole thing is crazy. Hell, she doesn't even know his name.

Adam is feeling just as torn inside. His biggest issue is their kiss, and more specifically the way she had kissed him *back*. It had been a kiss full of longing and need. It had been a kiss full of want. It had NOT been an angry get off me reaction, hitting him on the chest, pushing him away, which is what one would expect considering he *is* her kidnapper. So why had she kissed him back like that? Why had she moaned, and pushed herself slightly against him? Why had he found her horny and wet and withering around like a wanting vixen, waiting and ready, when he had come back from the store, after having cuffed her there in *anger*? His cock twitches at the thought, and he curses himself, looking at her out of the corner of his eyes. She is so damn fine, and seems so vulnerable curled up on the couch, he can't shake the idea of taking her in his arms and protecting her from all of this, holding her close, kissing her, and letting the rest unfold. When this is all over, he's going home to jerk off until he's spent.

The silence keeps dragging on and on and the tension grows worse. Adam and Demi still aren't talking to each other, they aren't even looking at each other, though they're sneaking glances out of the corner of their eyes, each hoping the other one won't be looking at the time. Both of their stomachs are in knots, eager to say something yet terrified to open their mouths out of fear of saying the wrong thing, or fear of saying too much.

When they hear Brandon's footsteps coming back down the hallway sometime later they both breathe a sigh of relief at the hopeful break in tension. But when he comes back in with his gun out, it takes them both by surprise, and Demi's breath catches in her throat. All feelings of sexual tension are gone between them now, replaced by fear and anxiety. No wonder they could hear his footsteps coming down the hallway so well. He's pissed off.

"Listen," he says to them, and while he's waving his gun off to the side, not pointed at anyone in particular, it still seems to command all of their attention. "I can't take this any longer. I need help making a better plan and getting control of things before they get any worse. You," he points to Adam with his free hand, "are coming with me while we sort this shit out. And you," he points now to Demi, "are going back into the bedroom. No funny business this time, in case you thought I wasn't being serious. I'm not in the mood for chase downs and tie ups." He waves the gun around to the side and then points his free hand towards the bedroom door, and Demi nods at him in agreement. She isn't eager to have that gun pointed at her.

She stands up and walks over to the small bedroom, not bothering to look at the younger one or at anything at all, keeping her eyes on the ground. She can hear the fridge open and shut behind her, and then there's some shuffling. Brandon comes into the bedroom behind her and hands her a bottle of water and a bag of chips before walking out and shutting and locking the door behind him. Hmm, she thinks to herself, he can't really be all that mad if he's still worrying about her accommodations, and he's likely got a bit more of a soft spot than he wants to admit.

Brandon holsters his gun and walks across the living room and back out into the hallway without a glance at Adam, or even a word of instruction for him either. He assumes that Adam will know well enough to follow, and to lock up behind himself. Adam is in no mood to poke at the beast right now, he knows better. He jumps up after Brandon and races after him out the doorway and then down the hall into the kitchen, leaving Demi locked up behind a double set of doors. At least this time she isn't cuffed up and begging to get off, he thinks with an embarrassed chuckle.

He is dying to know what's got Brandon all rattled, he wonders if it's just the situation in general or if something else has happened. Maybe Brandon was able to get a hold of her mother during his phone calls, but he knows better than to ask questions, and so he keeps his mouth shut until they reach the kitchen. He waits until Brandon sits down at the kitchen table first to follow suit, feeling nervous, like he's walking on eggshells.

He watches Brandon reach over to the junk drawer, open it, pull out a pack of smokes and light one up, and that's how Adam knows that Brandon is seriously stressing out. Neither of them are smokers, but Brandon's known to smoke a few when he's been drinking, or when he's under a lot of pressure.

Adam can't bite his tongue anymore, and he has to ask, "OK, so what's the news now?" "Nothing!" Brandon almost shouts at him in response, "I'm stressed out and just about ready to lose it right now, and I'm pissed off that nothing is going our way! That bitch isn't home, she's not at the hotel, I can't even guarantee that *is* the hotel she's staying at, and there's not even any trace of her that I can contact right now. I can't take all this time off work without raising suspicion, especially if things continue to drag on and on, I have to deal with that train ticket, which I shouldn't have even bought. What a stupid move. We aren't prepared for her to be here until Thursday, like hell, what if it's even longer..." Brandon trails off, stubbing out one smoke and then instantly lighting another.

Even though Adam doesn't often smoke, he reaches out and grabs the pack from the table and lights one up himself. He'd rather a joint, but he has a feeling this is about to get tense, and he'll take whatever stress reliever he can get his hands on right now. He lights it up and feels the need to take a page from Brandon's book and crack a joke to make things a little less awkward. "Well then, let's stop sitting around and whining like little women and let's make a plan of action that will get us through until then."

He isn't sure where this burst of confidence came from, but he's proud of himself. Someone needs to take control of the situation before Brandon ends up snapping and doing something stupid. And it's not like Adam has been in charge much before this, so it's time he's done something useful. He can't have Brandon checking out permanently, Adam can't handle this himself, and he doesn't want to be the leader. Brandon gives him a sideways look, taken back by Adam's words, but he's grateful for them, because he knows it too. Adam isn't the only one who's realized Brandon needs to kick his funk. "Alright then," Brandon replies, "help me."

The guys spend a few minutes going over some game plans for the week. They will need to make one more trip out and get a bigger supply of food and maybe a bit more clothes, but at a different store this time, just in case. And not together this time either. That had not been a very smart move. Brandon is working the afternoon shift this week, so they will have to take turns watching her. They don't plan to tell her about Brandon being at work though, thinking that it will be better if they make her think the guys are just breaking up their watch and can come back at any moment. Adam will take off in the early mornings, spend some time alone, do whatever he needs to do and keep the same profile he usually does. He will come back before Brandon's shift and then Brandon will leave for work and return by bedtime. Adam is not thrilled by the thought of being alone here with her for hours at a time, but at this point he doesn't really have much choice. It's not like he's going to speak up and tell Brandon that he isn't feeling man enough to handle being alone with her, and not capable of doing the job he's here to do. And he *knows* that Brandon's right, they don't want to arouse suspicions later on either.

After a little while the guys have had a chance to talk everything over and they feel a lot less tense about the situation, though it's still not ideal, and Brandon has calmed down significantly. He's going to be the one to go out and get the rest of their supplies and go to the train station and leave Adam there for a half hour to an hour or so to get started on dinner. When Brandon comes back to the farm house he'll make a few more phone calls and then they can all have dinner together and then wait.

Tomorrow Brandon will go to work for his afternoon shift and will go again Tuesday and Wednesday as well if need be. He is going to call in sick Thursday, because by then this will all be over with. He just knows it. This can't possibly drag on any longer than Thursday, right? If they haven't heard from her mother by then, Brandon is going to lose it. He goes on to make a few more points about the next couple of days, but Adam is having a hard time following anymore. He's lost in his thoughts again, thinking about all of that time he's going to be spending alone with her, and how he's ever going to manage.

Demi sits alone on the cot in the tiny quiet bedroom. She forces herself to breathe deeply and listen to the silence, settling her body and stilling her mind. It has been a very crazy and emotional day for her, and she wants to spend this time wisely, regrouping herself so she can think properly, and sort of prepare herself for what's coming. Her mind is ready to race with all sorts of thoughts and questions she doesn't have answers for, thoughts about her mother and their past together, thoughts about how she really feels about her mother taking this extra vacation, or all of her vacations in general, thoughts about the kidnapping, and questions like what will happen if her mother doesn't get the message and doesn't come back until Thursday? What if she doesn't come back until even later, and doesn't even know Demi's been kidnapped or knows to send these guys any money? What if her mother doesn't come to save her? Will she have to rescue herself? Can she rescue herself?

She forces some more deep slow breaths into her and pushes these scary thoughts away as they pop into her mind. She continues to concentrate on the silence around her. It will only be a matter of time before the guys come back and things get awkward again, or tense, or sexually stressful between her and the younger one, and she wants to enjoy not feeling horny or embarrassed or stressed out or any emotions really, for just a minute. She just wants to enjoy being alone with herself. She may not have any idea what the future holds, but she knows what this moment holds for her right now, if she'll let it, and that's peace and quiet and stillness.

Adam finds himself puttering around in the kitchen, having a hard time focusing on what he's cooking, or anything else he's supposed to be doing. His head is a mess. He keeps seeing her right there in front of him, seeing himself reaching out for her, feeling her soft skin under his hand, remembering her touch and her taste. He keeps feeling her warm wet lips pressing against his, kissing him back eagerly. She had kissed him with so much longing, and that is his biggest problem and the one thing he just can't stop thinking about, next to the scene of her handcuffed and horny on the cot. And those two things have to be related somehow, he knows it.

If only she had pushed him away, yelled at him, called him an asshole, gotten angry with him, something negative, then maybe he would be able to let it go. Instead he just keeps running his tongue over his lips, tasting her, and imagining what the rest of her tastes like, and what it would be like to have his way with her. Would she be so eager if he'd taken her when he'd found her in the bedroom? Would she still kiss him with such an urgency and need, and press against him desperately, when it was more than her mouth he was taking?

He's so lost in his thoughts that when Brandon comes through the door to the carport and it bangs shut behind him, Adam shouts, jumps and reaches for his gun. "Easy there, killer," Brandon says laughing, and sets the bags down by the table, beginning to put things away. "What are you making for us?" Brandon walks over to the stove and eyes up Adam's concoction of easy meals and finger foods, not much different from what they'd had for a quick lunch. "Not much of a chef huh, maybe I should have sent you to the store instead. How are you two going to feed yourselves when I am at work every night?"

Brandon laughs again at his own joke and eyes Adam up when he doesn't share in his humor. "Just make sure you two are not feeding each other in other ways." Now Adam does laugh, mostly because he's embarrassed and needs to break the mood. "Common man," he replies, "give it a rest, or I'm going to think you're the one that's secretly in love with her and you're just jealous of me and her or something." This gets both of the guys laughing together and it breaks up the tension between them a little bit. Brandon helps him finish making dinner and they prep the plates and cutlery and pile everything onto the tray and into their arms. The guys make their way back into the living room, locking up the door behind them.

Adam takes a seat back on the same couch where he had been sitting before. He sets the tray of food on the coffee table and begins to set up dinner while Brandon sets the stack of plates and silverware he is carrying down beside the tray and goes and unlocks the small bedroom door for Demi. She'd heard them come into the living room and was ready for them to return, desperately hoping that they will open up the door and let her out, or she is about to start banging. This tiny room does not have a bathroom, and she lets Brandon know that as soon as he greets her at the door. Brandon gives her a half ass apology and follows it up with a little chuckle and lets her slip past him and run into the washroom.

Brandon takes a seat on the couch, choosing to sit beside Adam to put some space between those two so that it might ease some of their anxiety around each other. Then he grabs the remote and turns on the TV. He's already sick of watching this stupid screen, not being a big TV person, but he searches for another movie anyway. He needs to suck it up and get used to it being on in here or it's going to be a very long few days. He settles on something that's fairly new, and they sit back and wait for her to join them.

Demi washes up and heads out of the bathroom. She takes a seat opposite the guys, and when Brandon nods at her and the food, they all begin to eat. She's had quite some time to relax and calm down, and now instead of anxiety or sexual tension or stress, she's actually feeling a little bit depressed and bummed, and she's really tired too. It's been a long day for her, and everything is catching up with her now. She is ready to eat and curl up and sleep right through until Thursday.

Adam can sense the change in her mood, but he has no idea what's caused it, though he worries it may have something to do with their kiss and not about the kidnapping at all. He wishes he didn't want to know. This girl has a crazy way of getting under his skin that's causing all sorts of feelings and confusion in him.

Brandon however, has no desire to see her so miserable and he also can't stand to feel the tension in the room arise again, not after he's worked so hard to make a new plan and figure things out so that they can get through this easily enough. He's determined to get her talking, especially because he wants to use this opportunity to get answers to a few more questions of his own and help put his mind at ease. He watches her eat for a bit, letting her get settled, and then Brandon asks her if she's in school or if she works, and what she typically does with her days.

Demi shrugs and swallows a mouthful of food before she speaks. For some reason, she doesn't feel as annoyed by the older guy asking her personal questions like she did when the younger one asked her earlier, so she doesn't get nearly as defensive with her answers this time. "I don't really do anything right now, as dumb or boring as that sounds. I floated around in college for a bit, but I couldn't find anything that I really wanted to concentrate or focus on, or that I actually *wanted* to do with my life. I tried my hand at a couple of odd jobs just to get out of the house, as clearly you guys know money isn't an issue for me or my family, but I'm obviously too flaky to hold one down. It's because I don't care about them, and they didn't interest me. Nothing really interests me these days. I know it sounds stupid, and cliché, but I don't really do anything with my life."

Neither Adam nor Brandon are about to tell her that it doesn't exactly sound cliché to two guys who don't work steady jobs, or have much formal education, and who don't really do anything with their lives either; two guys whose most exciting act in life lately had been to kidnap her for money.

"Well then, do you go out with your girlfriends a lot, tear up the town, do you have a boyfriend, or maybe a girlfriend?" Brandon asks next and wiggles an eyebrow at her with a smirk. The wiggle gets to her and she lets out a good laugh, holding her stomach, and the sound of her laugh mixed with the thought of her possible answer stops Adams breath in his throat for two reasons, and neither make him feel good. The first is that he didn't have the nerve to ask her about having a boyfriend earlier, and he still isn't ready to hear her answer if it's a yes. The second is that her laughing at Brandon's jokes and comedy acts like that are cutting into him like a knife. He's green with envy over his buddy, and he knows he's being absolutely ridiculous. But she's just so comfortable and at ease with Brandon and yet so tense and uptight with Adam, he can't help it.

That plus the thought of her having a boyfriend is killing him right now, and if she says yes, he also doesn't know if he's going to be able to control his face or what may come out of his mouth. He bites his tongue and clenches his hands into tight fists, trying to calm himself. He also can't stand the thought of Demi and Brandon being alone during the mornings and Brandon making her laugh like that anymore. Because all he can do is cause her to be uncomfortable. These thoughts of jealousy are coming out of nowhere, taking him by surprise, and they're very overwhelming. He needs to get himself together.

"I have no close girlfriends," she says with a sad laugh, bringing Adam back to the conversation in front of him, "and I don't really have a lot of good friends, or even friends either. Mostly just acquaintances that I check in with from time to time, or who check in with me. I don't go to the clubs or the bars, in fact the few beers I have had with you guys today are more than I've drank in a long time. And I know what you're getting at with all of your questions. I don't really have an active social life at all, and I highly doubt anyone is going to notice me missing for a few days." Hearing herself say that out loud only reinforces the crappy downer feelings that are creeping in. She is all alone.

And those feelings intensify when Brandon tells her that that's actually for the best, as it won't interfere with their plans. "If anything, I need your mother to be the one that goes to your house and finds the ransom note, not one of your concerned girlfriends or a boyfriend who might report you missing. I need to be the one to speak with her directly, before she speaks to anyone else. I don't want the cops to get involved, I don't want this to equal any kind of jail time for my buddy and I, I just want this to go exactly as it was supposed to from the start, a simple exchange of you for money, and then you can go back to your mother, and your normal life."

Demi is feeling really, *really* flustered by all of this. The older one sure has a way of speaking so casually about something that's so hard for her to comprehend; she had been kidnapped last night! She's being held for ransom, and her life is upside down right now! And her mother, who is supposed to rescue her, is off who knows where chasing the sunset. And it doesn't even matter how she feels about any of this. How can all of that be something that goes so unnoticed by the mastermind of the kidnapping?

Slowly, the feelings of sadness and depression she has inside of her begin to boil into anger. She's nothing but an amount of money to these guys, her mother's money, and that money is supposed to be left to her and her mother after her father died. Now it's just being taken from them, and to make it worse, she's nothing more than a pawn in it all! She's so angry with her mother, who doesn't even give a shit about her, off vacationing again like always, spending their money by the boatload and never even bothering to check in to see if Demi's doing OK. Her mother is supposed to be the one rescuing her, and she doesn't even know anything is wrong.

And Demi's mad that she's clearly still not mentally stable, and that she's been acting like such a horny slut this whole time because of her sexually repressed issues. She's mad at the younger one for having kissed her in the first place, but she's even more angry at herself for giving in and kissing him back, she should have pushed him away.

But mostly though, she's just really upset that her father died, and she's missing him like crazy. She's been so broken up over it since it happened, she hasn't got any kind of closure yet, and she realizes that none of this would be happening if he was still alive, or, if she had moved on from his death, moved out and had not been there to be kidnapped in the first place.

She takes another deep breath, trying to calm herself. She eyes up the gun on the older guys hip, and it gets her thinking about his temper too. A gun paired with his ability to blow at any time could be bad news if this drags on too long, or if something unexpected happens, or if she says the wrong thing, or if he finds out something happened between her and the other one. She thinks she's safe, but for how long? She can't help questioning that anymore. There are far too many what ifs to this situation, and all of it only adds to her depression, and her anxiety.

As the night begins to draw to a close, their anxious moods cause the room to grow tense again, with all of them lost in their own thoughts, their own uncertainties, what ifs and questions. The TV continues to run an old movie in the background, but no one is really paying any attention anymore. If the phone doesn't ring soon, they are going to have to call it quits for the day, and hope for something different tomorrow.

Adam isn't sure if there has ever been a day in his life that has passed as slowly as this one. He is more than eager to get to bed and get this over with, but at the same time, he doesn't really want to be away from her for a second. And that's exactly why he *needs* to get away from her. Catch 22. He can't control the way he keeps looking at her out of the corner of his eye, he can't stop seeing that scene in the bedroom over and over in his head, he can't stop tasting her on his lips, and he hates himself for it. He knows that he's ran this same thought through his head a hundred times today and it's pathetic and stupid. He's only driving himself crazy.

He keeps telling himself there is nothing special about her even though he doesn't believe it, he tells himself that she's a manipulative broken girl who would never ever be interested in him. He tells himself that even though her kiss tells him otherwise, he is her kidnapper and she would never like him like that. Adam grows miserable, trying to desperately concentrate on the movie in front of him, and shut his rambling mind down.

Brandon can't even stand to be in the living room anymore. He doesn't know if it's because of Adam and Demi or if it's his temper wearing thin at this whole situation, but he is ready to explode. He's never been so grateful to see the clock tick closer and closer to bedtime in all of his adult life. Try as he may, he can't break the tension here, and if Demi's mother isn't going to call today, he's done with it. Between Demi moping around here this evening half depressed, Adam sitting around here halfcocked and ready for her, staring at her with lust in his puppy dog eyes, and whatever weird sexual tension those two have going on, on top of the kidnapping gone wrong, it's enough to make him want to scream.

When the movie they are currently watching finally comes to an end and the credits begin to roll on the screen, Brandon damn near leaps up from the couch. "Alright," he calls out, jumping up and clapping his hands. "Time to call it a day. Let's try this charade again tomorrow, and hope for better luck. Though don't you think for a second that I won't have this phone on and loud all night, just in case. You my dear," he points to Demi, and then to the bathroom, "should go use the washroom and do whatever you have to do before bed, and then I'm locking you up for the night again. No hard feelings doll, I'm just making sure all of the bases are covered here. I sleep like a rock. And well, this guy," he points to Adam, "can be just as bad."

Brandon means it as a joke, but Demi jumps up at his orders, her whole body tense, planning to do exactly as she's told. Somehow the seriousness of this hadn't sunk in for her yet until just now; her mother hasn't called for her, she's still kidnapped, and everything is out of her control. She's going back to sleep on that cot in that tiny little closet like bedroom, and wait for another day, hoping to be rescued then.

Demi forces herself to laugh at his joke, although it's a meek attempt at laughter, and then she walks to the bathroom and shuts the door behind her. She can feel the tears threatening, and she doesn't have the strength to fight them anymore, nor does she want to cry in front of the guys again either. So alone in the bathroom she lets them fall, sitting herself down on the floor against the shower, silently crying and hugging herself tightly. She knows she probably doesn't have a long time before one of them comes asking what's taking her so long, and she knows she'll be alone soon enough in the bedroom, but she can't help taking a few minutes now to let the tears out and let herself feel what she needs to feel. It's been a very emotional day. She's tired. And she's ready for it all to be over with.

Demi gives herself a minute or two longer, then she picks herself up off of the floor, tells herself she's strong enough, and that she can do this with *or* without her mother. She brushes her teeth, washes her face, and then uses the washroom and washes up. When she thinks she's ready, she takes a deep breath and opens the door, feeling a strange sense of Deja vu, almost expecting Adam to be in the doorway when she opens the door. But he isn't, and she feels a touch of disappointment, and annoyance with herself, at feeling like that.

While she's been in the bathroom, the guys have moved things around a little bit for Adam again. They've pulled the coffee table and TV away from between the two couches, so they could pull the one couch out, and the younger one is slowly making it up with blankets and getting himself settled for bed. The older guy is over at the small bedrooms open door, once again waiting for her. She takes another deep breath and walks across the living room, not making eye contact with the younger one, and then passes through the doorway into the makeshift room. She turns to her captor and Brandon hands her a bottle of water and begins to shut the door for the night, without saying a word. Through the closing door, she can't help but make eye contact now with the one sitting on the pull out, and she feels her heart skip a beat.

"Wait!" She yells, quickly ripping her gaze away and turning to Brandon. She hadn't meant to cry out like that, but she's scared, and conflicted, and she just opened her mouth and it came out. She stumbles for a second on what to say next, and then recovers. "What if I have to use the washroom again, or I need another drink or something in the middle of the night? I mean, common, you guys are armed for Pete's sake, and you can't really be that heavy of sleepers." She fidgets with the water bottle in her hand while she talks. She doesn't know where this desperation has come from, she just knows she doesn't want him to shut that door and lock her in here alone for the night.

Brandon gives her a look, and for a moment she thinks he might actually cave and let her sleep with the door open. She feels a faint spark of hope ignite inside of her, but then it's extinguished just as quickly as Brandon shuts the door in her face and she hears the lock click into place on the other side. "She thinks I'm a softy." Brandon says, laughing, and then he crosses the living room to the bedroom and begins to get himself ready for bed.

Despite all of the turmoil building up inside him, Adam forces himself to bite his tongue at Brandon's remark. He knows that saying anything against the locked door right now will open one hell of a can of worms, but he does feel bad for her being shut up in there all night. It sure has been a crazy day for them all, and technically it hasn't even been a full 24 hours yet for that poor girl; her head must be an absolute mess, he thinks to himself. But then again, he isn't supposed to care about her, and he hates the fact that she's somehow gotten this far under his skin. He is her kidnapper, and the deal is she's supposed to be locked up. He needs to get it together.

He also needs to get some sleep tonight and forget about all of these crazy feelings. He is passed exhausted at this point, and clearly not thinking straight. Tomorrow he will have some time away from all of this and he can try and get his head sorted then. Maybe it will all be over with tomorrow anyway.

Except nothing's been working out in their favor today, so why should Adam be graced with the sleep he desperately needs? Brandon is out of the bathroom, tucked into the bigger bedroom with the door left open and snoring away within 20 minutes. But for Adam, it's like all of a sudden, he isn't even tired anymore. His mind wants to race, but he refuses to let himself think about anything, trying to push all of his unwanted thoughts away. He lays there breathing heavily while he listens to Brandon snoring away in the other room, and the occasional squeak of the cot from the tiny bedroom as he hears her rolling around and around in there. He finds himself wishing that Brandon had shut his bedroom door, but he either doesn't trust him or doesn't trust the situation, or maybe it's a little bit of both. At least *someone* is sleeping like a baby tonight though, Adam thinks enviously.

He hears the cot squeak again, and then again. He can't exactly blame Demi for not being able to sleep either. With everything going on, and that tiny uncomfortable bed she's laying on, she's probably in there crying herself to sleep, or curled up in a little ball, scared. Or...

Adam can't stop himself, thinking about her laying on that cot brings the scene from earlier today back into his mind, and then his thoughts are spiraling away from him before he can get a handle on them; Demi handcuffed and stretched out across that cot, so hot, wet and horny at *her* own doing. And it had to all be a mental thing as she wasn't exactly able to touch herself, she would have had to settle with rubbing her legs together desperately, getting nothing but a little pressure from her thighs.

He wonders what had been playing in her head at the time, what had she been thinking about that had distracted her from the seriousness of being kidnapped and turned her into a panting horny school girl. Adam has a feeling that his hands all over her, dominating her, holding her down, pinning her and cuffing her up had something to do with it. This whole situation must touch a nerve in her, setting her off somewhere deep inside. Maybe she has some kinky sides to her yet to truly be explored being so young, Adam finds himself thinking, and this brushes on that fantasy. Because don't lots of women have a fantasy of being held down and dominated, yet not hurt?

These thoughts are driving him mad, and they aren't helping his current situation. Adam is hard as a rock, he's been so hard all day it's almost painful. Yet he just doesn't feel right about masturbating; not with Brandon's door wide open, complete with sound effects, and the conflicting feelings he's having about everything in general. But he can't shake the thought of release, nor can he get rid of his cravings for her, and so he continues to roll around on the squeaky pull out, settling for being achy and miserable, hoping for sleep to eventually pull him under.

Demi isn't any better off than he is right now. She rolls around and around on the tiny cot, unable to get comfortable, listening to the faint snoring of the older guy in the far bedroom, and the sounds of the pull-out couch in the living room. The constant squeaking as he rolls over and over gives her an odd sense of comfort. She is not the only one up restless and confused.

She doesn't understand it, but Demi is drawn to him in some stupid way, and she thinks he may be as well, or else why has he been so weird and moody, and what else would explain that kiss, and the way he had been so hands on with her, dominating her, cuffing her to the bed? If he had simply kissed her in the moment, or had been acting like a typical horny guy, it wouldn't still be awkward, or dragging on and on like this. There just seems to be so many signs that point to the same confusion and uncertainty that she's feeling herself.

Her thoughts drift back to the feel of his strong hands all over her again; he's clearly had some experience with this, she thinks to herself, he had pulled the authority card with her no problem, and he'd shown zero hesitation at all while holding her, pinning her and punishing her when he needed to. He could just as easily have pulled his gun out, pointed it at her, and ordered her onto the bed. Why get hands on and touch her like that, and cuff her up?

Her thoughts are racing all over the place. Part of her mind wants to drift back into her slump, and feel depressed about the situation and her mother and her life, but most of her can't stop thinking about that tattooed hunk laying out there on the pull-out, and what it would be like if he were to open that door right now, come inside the bedroom and climb on that little cot beside her, and get on top of her. The thought makes her stomach tighten, and she pushes her thighs together, feeling herself grow wet and tingly. Her body is screaming out in need for him, aching for him.

In her fantasy world, there are no questions, and so it doesn't matter one way or another why she lets him into her bed. She imagines she does just that, and then he's there with her in her mind. She remembers the feeling of his lips on hers, and his tongue pushing its way into her mouth. She can't help herself now, this time her arms aren't cuffed up, and she doesn't have to be teased endlessly, even by herself. She has no problem reaching down between her legs and slipping her hand underneath her panties. She is so wet, and her middle finger glides around easily, lightly rubbing her clit as she imagines herself pretending to get away from him. He'd force her down again, tell her that she was such a bad girl, cuff her up, and punish her and pleasure her all at once. She rolls over onto her stomach and rubs her clit harder, then slides her fingers deep inside of her and back up to her clit, feeling her juices pool into her hand as the thought of being used by him, willingly, makes her cum hard. She moans quietly into the pillow, hoping that no one hears her, grateful for that final release she needed so badly.

She only regrets her decision for a moment afterwards, when she remembers she can't use the washroom to clean herself up, but then she recalls the bottle of water and the laundry in the corner, and it will have to do. It's not like she's the one that has to clean up later anyway, and the release was a long time coming. And hey, it's not like she's squeaky clean either, one hillbilly bath won't kill her, she thinks. She crawls back into bed after and begins the same restless tossing and turning that Adam is, and eventually falls into a miserable sleep filled with thoughts of running away in the darkness, feeling scared, and her mother not returning for her, leaving her with a general sense of loss and abandonment.

Chapter Ten
Monday Morning

When Demi wakes up after a terrible sleep, she feels groggy, moody and downright melancholy. She can see a faint light under the crack of the door and hears a few sounds coming from the other room; nothing specific, but she has a feeling it's getting close to morning time, and as tired and grumpy and depressed as she's feeling, she knows she's not going to get anymore sleep. She is dying to use the washroom, and she silently curses the older guy for being so picky about locking her in. She goes back to the same tossing and turning of the night before, but this morning she's lacking all of that sexual energy, now she's just waiting for someone to release her from her prison.

Demi is not the only one who spent the evening rolling around in bed. Adam tossed and turned the night away himself, dreaming about fighting with Brandon over the money, about everything going wrong, dreaming about coming on to her and her rejecting him, hell, he'd even dreamed about her getting away from him somehow and that he screwed the whole thing up over a stupid crush. All in all, it was one of the worst night's sleep of his life, and he's about ready to leave for the morning, just for a break from the entire thing.

Adam runs his hands through his hair and sighs. He lies awake for a few minutes, slowing his breath and trying to prepare himself for what lies ahead today. Very shortly, he'll be packing up and leaving, and Brandon and Demi will spend hours alone together, laughing, bonding, killing time, while he very likely drives around aimlessly, putters around in his apartment, and maybe takes a nap and jerks off in the shower.

He hasn't made plans for the day yet and doesn't even care to, he hasn't really been able to think about much of anything or concentrate at all since yesterday.

The longer he lies here, the more irritated and agitated he's going to become, and he knows it. Plus, there are still a few more minutes left before he knows Brandon's alarm is set to go off. He can't stay in bed any longer, thinking about what lies ahead, and he's feeling eager to do something, so he gets up and gets dressed and then uses the washroom quietly and leaves the living room. He heads down the hallway to the kitchen to make coffee, being sure to lock the door behind him.

He takes his time in the kitchen, thinking about what's to come. More specifically, he is trying to focus on what he can do today, how he's going to keep himself busy, and not think about the upcoming evening when it will be his turn to be alone with her for hours. He doesn't know how he's going to get through it, let alone day after day if this drags on until Thursday. But at the same time, he isn't exactly eager for her mother to call and for her to leave yet, either.

It's twenty minutes later when he finally makes his way back down the hallway with the tray of coffee, mugs, sugar and cream, and he feels a little more relaxed about the situation. At least he does until he gets to the door of the living room. He sets the tray down on the floor to unlock the door and he hears her laugh behind it. Another twinge of jealousy forms in the pit of his stomach, catching him off guard, and once again he tells himself that he's being ridiculous and tries to push the feeling away. He knows that of the two of them, Brandon is much more professional when it comes to matters of the heart and sex vs business, being far more motivated by money, and yet he can't help but think about the way Brandon's made a few sexual jokes and comments and wiggled his eyebrows at her. And clearly, he can make her laugh, whereas Adam only adds to the sexual tension and weirdness they have going on between them.

Demi watches Adam come in the living room, trying to hide a scowl on his face, and she notices that he seems awfully rough looking and miserable. He's probably about as tired as she looks and feels, Demi thinks to herself. The older one had let her out of the room a little while earlier, and she's had a chance to get dressed, wash her face and try to freshen up as best as she can, but she knows she looks terrible from the last few restless nights; the toll is starting to show on her. Between the first night's late-night kidnapping after an already restless sleep, and then last night's emotional tossing and turning fest, she feels like she's been put through the wringer and hung up to dry.

Before the younger one had come back into the room, the older one had been telling her a joke about a former roofing job that he had held in the past, and something to do with the co-workers there. It had been a nice distraction for her from what's really going on. Brandon starts over to fill Adam in on it, hoping that making him feel included will lighten up Adam's grumpy mood a little bit. He is not dealing with his mopey attitude this morning, and if Adam is going to keep it up, he is more than welcome to leave.

Adam takes a seat on the couch opposite of them, taking note of the room around him. Brandon, or more likely both Brandon and Demi together, have put the couch away and tidied the room up, and now the two of them are sitting almost touching each other on the couch. Adam is tired of telling himself that it's all in his head and that he doesn't have any right to be jealous anyway; he knows that he's right, but he's simply tired of it.

The longer he sits there though, drinking his coffee and listening to them chat, chiming in half ass like when he absolutely needs to, he begins to drive himself crazy. He almost feels like a third wheel here, the way he's withdrawn and closed himself off, and by the way they are so casual and at ease with each other.

He is torn with the want to leave as soon as possible, and then the need to stay for every single moment and not miss a thing. He listens as Brandon informs her about their plans for the week, trying to keep himself calm. He tells her that until her mother calls when she gets the emergency message, or until she gets home and finds the ransom note, the guys are going to start taking shifts, alternating between hanging out with her and leaving to take care of some other things going on in their lives. "Things you don't need to know about," he adds, wagging a finger at her jokingly, "So don't you ask." And Demi finds herself retorting right back at him "Just like your names huh?"

Adam laughs at this. He laughs so hard he almost spits out his coffee, and even still, he manages to spill some on the knee of his jeans. The laugh catches the other two off guard, and in return Demi and Brandon end up letting out a laugh too. The joke and shared laughter totally breaks Adams grumpy mood, and it helps release some of the tension that followed him into the room. "Well," Brandon replies to her, "Why don't you just call me Brad, for Brad Pitt, because I'm just so damn smooth and good looking." This gets Demi and Adam laughing even harder, and laughing together, sharing a moment, and when they lock eyes mid laugh it breaks down the tension that's been building between them tremendously.

"What," Brandon questions them accusingly, pretending to be hurt. "You guys don't think I have Hollywood good looks?" Adam shakes his head at his friend, still laughing, "No, not even close!" Adam and Demi try to get their giggles under control while Brandon looks at them with pretend hurt on his face. "You guys just don't appreciate me, fine, I get it."

Once they're settled down again, Demi yawns and stretches her legs out in front of her, tired, realizing how cramped and tight her muscles and body feels. Sitting so close beside her, Brandon notices her grimace and hears her joints crack and pop, and his heart moves a bit for her. "Hey," Brandon says to her, nudging her gently with his elbow, "Maybe if you're good I'll take you out back with my gun and let you run around for a little bit."

This gets her laughing again, her stomach hurting now, but it only causes Adam's mood to shift once more. He isn't sure he can sit around and deal with much more of this, her happy laughter is killing him, his jealousy of those two is out of control, and he needs some fresh air and to get out, *now*. Adam jumps up from the couch while she's still laughing, and he downs the rest of his coffee in one big gulp. "Well, I guess I should get going, it's my turn first." he says awkwardly, and begins to grab some of his things from behind the couch before waiting for a reply. He's almost at the door before Brandon speaks up from behind him, talking to his back. "Alright man, have a good one, and don't forget to be back at the time we talked about earlier so that I can get out and get some stuff done too."

Adam knows Brandon works at 3, which means Adam needs to be back here by 2. Which is so far away and yet not nearly long enough. And it bothers him so very much that Demi hasn't said a word to him, though it's not like he's said goodbye to her either. "Will do," Adam replies, and walks out and locks the door behind him, without glancing back nor looking at Demi as he goes. He can't take it.

Chapter Eleven:
Monday, Adam's Morning and Afternoon

Adam leaves the house in a hurry, locking the kitchen door behind him, making sure not to slam it out of his sudden burst of anger. He stands still for a moment, enjoying the fresh air and silence, and being out of the room, then he rounds the house to his truck. He gets in and sits there for a few minutes, breathing deeply, trying to wrap his head around everything that's happened in the past day and a half. Nothing has turned out the way it was supposed to. Right now, the guys should have been long gone, Brandon on his way to an island, or on a holiday vacation or whatever he had planned. And Adam, well, who knows. Maybe he'd just be sitting around in his apartment, miserable, a million dollars richer.

Adam can't believe that he still hasn't put any thought into what he's going to do once this is all over with. He's going to be a millionaire and be able to do anything he wants with his life. Yet he's too distracted with what's happening right now with her here in front of him.

There is a small part of him that's worried about the police, and jail time. Adam knows he is not made for prison. But for the most part he pushes those thoughts aside. From what Brandon's researched and found out about the girl and her family, and from what she's told them herself, she is a loaner. A few days off the radar is not going to raise any alarms in her life. It does seem like a pretty fool proof plan.

He sighs heavily. Right now, he just wants to be alone and away from her and every single thing about this situation so that he can think. He can't think there, not around her, or Brandon. Or at least he can't think about what he wants to think about; all his mind wants to focus on is her, her cuffed up, her legs spread for him, moaning, wet, and her kissing him back with such passion and urgency. He didn't sleep last night, his appetite is awful, and he can't concentrate on anything Brandon says, or the plans. He can't even trust or promise himself that he won't screw this up, he already can't believe he kissed her. What if she had kissed him back and grabbed the gun while doing so?

He smacks his fists off the dashboard in frustration, telling himself to just let it go and leave it all behind him for a few hours, because this is his opportunity to do so. He's angry with himself for acting like this, and feeling stuck, but it takes him another ten minutes still to start his truck. There is a voice screaming at him inside of his head, telling him that leaving Demi and Brandon alone is a bad idea, and that when he comes back he'll find the two of them cuddled up together and they'll be making plans for their future. He sees that exact scene run through his mind, and the thought of Brandon snuggling up with anyone, let alone a woman he sees as business and dollar signs, makes him laugh. That sort of lifts his spirits again, and he tells himself that he's just being ridiculous, and forces himself to drive around the house and down the driveway without looking back.

Adam has no plans or destination in mind, and he ends up touring around aimlessly for almost an hour before he drives back to his apartment, pissed off at himself for having wasted all of that time. He unlocks his door and wanders in, taken aback by the quiet and stillness after all the tension at the farm house. He walks around his place in circles, packs up a bag of extra clothes without giving much thought to what he's grabbing, and tosses the bag in the corner by the door for when he's ready to go.

Then he forces himself to jump in the shower. He's been restless all day, and he knows that a lot of his restlessness comes from sexual frustration; the amount of times that Demi's sexy body has gone through his head in the last day and a half, the amount of hard ons he's sported, a good jerk off will do him some good. And it doesn't take him long under the hot heat of the shower, with some slippery soap, finally enjoying all the thoughts of her he's been denying himself. He imagines her pussy is as tight and slippery and wet as his fist feels right now, and after a few long slow strokes, thoughts of her send him over the edge, and he releases a thick stream of cum onto the shower floor and then down the drain.

He stays in the shower until the water goes cold. After, he gets dressed and grabs his newly packed bag, puts on a hat, locks up and gets back in his truck. His apartment feels so quiet and empty and he can't stand to stay here either. He's too wired to sleep, and he's far too much of a mess to sit still. So, he stops at a gas station and fills the tank, and then he puts on the radio and just drives. Adam stops a few times for coffee, otherwise he cranks the music to keep his mind clear of any thoughts other than the lyrics of songs and the road in front of him.

Adam doesn't lose track of time, but he also doesn't let the ticking clock stress him out, now that he's out and about and feeling slightly more relaxed, he's going to force himself to make the most of it, because who knows what the night holds for him, and for them.

Eventually, the time on the dashboard of his truck shows him it's not too long before Brandon has to leave for work. Adam is cutting it close, but he turns into a fast food joint anyway for some burgers and fries for them all before heading back to the house. He pulls his truck up the driveway and around back again, killing the engine. He takes a couple deep breaths, prepares himself for what's ahead, and then grabs his backpack and the bags of food and heads into the house.

Chapter Twelve:
Monday Early Evening

Adam wanders into the living room with his bags and locks the door behind him to find Brandon and Demi pretty much where he left them. The pair of them are curled up on the couch watching TV, and they both look happy and relaxed. He refuses to let this affect him.

"Holy man," Brandon says to him, looking up from the TV and clicking it off, annoyance in his voice, "you didn't exactly leave me much time you know." Adam shrugs and mumbles sorry in way of an apology and leaves it at that. He walks over and sets the bags of food down on the coffee table, then he tosses his backpack in the corner and takes a seat on the couch across from them. "He didn't leave you much time for what?" Demi asks Brandon questioningly, but she gets no reply. She wasn't expecting one.

Adam doesn't really speak to either of them, he just digs into one of the bags of food and pulls out a burger and chows down. Demi watches the older one help himself to a burger as well, and then he gets up and starts grabbing his coat and getting himself ready to go. Demi feels her stomach tighten in anticipation of what's about to come. She's known all day long that he was going to leave her alone with the younger one, but she kept hoping for some reason it wouldn't happen. And now, it's happening. And she has no idea what the evening holds.

The older guy gives them both a nod and pulls out his keys and heads for the living room door. "I'll be back in a few hours. Don't do anything stupid." He says with a laugh, and then he walks out, locking the door behind him and leaving Demi and Adam alone.

The room falls silent other than the sounds of Adam eating. For the most part, earlier in the day they'd been playing cards and board games with the TV turned off, but the mood between Demi and the older one is always light and easy, so they don't need that added distraction, plus he'd let her know that he wasn't a fan of the TV. There doesn't seem to be the tension and sexual frustration that her and the younger one share, and it's no wonder why. The older one is professional, and he's in control of himself, and not broken inside.

With the younger one now, however, the second they make eye contact her stomach tightens up and her thighs want to do the same against the throbbing between her legs. He does something stupid to her, and it's been such a struggle to get her mind off of that throughout the day she'd spent with the older one. The anticipation of this coming evening has drove her crazy all day long, and now she's living in it, and it's just as stressful and tense and sexually charged as she knew it would be. She can't stand the silence any longer, and doesn't want to get sucked into her head, so she takes control, grabbing the TV remote and flipping it on and picking a movie for them to watch and then she takes a box of fries and a chicken burger from the bag and begins to eat.

The tension in the room and between them only continues to build though as the afternoon passes. A few times they both open their mouth to say something to each other and then stop themselves, not really knowing what to say, nor wanting to be the first one to speak, and so the silence drags on and the tension just gets heavier, with both of them thinking that this is going to be a very long evening.

Eventually they finish eating, and Demi feels compelled to start piling the garbage together and begin cleaning up, just to give herself something to do. "You don't have to do that, I can," Adam says, finally breaking the silence between them. He reaches over and takes one of the brown bags from her, and their fingers brush accidentally, sending sparks flying. They both do a quick dump of their garbage and then Adam takes the bags and crumples them into a ball, and he walks over to the can in the corner by the beer fridge and tosses them out. He's feeling a little more back to normal and in control of himself now, and when he sits down and starts talking to her, the words come out easily, although he is ashamed to say he's somewhat embarrassed at what he says, and the way he's feeling.

"I'm sorry I've made things really awkward around here. That's on me, but I don't honestly have an explanation for the way I have acted or what I've done. I guess," he trails off for a minute, thinking about that bedroom scene for a moment, and then laughs, a real belly laugh, breaking the tension a bit. "I guess seeing you like that in the bedroom just caught me off guard. And then, I don't know, things just sort of escalated from there. I didn't mean to kiss you, I just uh, I just couldn't help myself I guess, right there in the moment, but I didn't mean to mess everything up either and cause you a bunch of unnecessary stress on top of what this kidnapping is probably already doing to you."

Demi feels herself blush. She's thankful he's opening up to her, for some reason that gives her more trust in him and helps bring her anxiety and guard down a little more. But it also gives her butterflies, lots and lots of them. He's just as confused as she is, that confirms it. The whole thing was never an act or something he had planned along with the kidnapping. It had happened spontaneously. He hadn't meant to hurt her or cause her grief, and he's worried about how she is doing. And while she doesn't understand or know how she feels about that kiss, she is definitely glad it happened.

Adam can't help but notice her blush, and as much as he hates to admit it, it makes him feel better inside. He's glad he let her know what he's feeling, and it also makes him happy to see that she clearly enjoyed hearing what he had to say. He takes a deep breath and almost lets out a sigh of relief, realizing just how much tension he's really been carrying the last little while. It feels good to let his guard down and relax with her a bit.

He risks sneaking another glance at Demi while she isn't looking and admires her for a minute. She has a lot of courage and a lot of spirit; she probably doesn't even realize how strong she really is. He catches himself day dreaming about her and mentally scolds himself. He's got to get out of his head before he ends up confessing his love for this poor girl. Regardless of how she may have blushed or reacted to the memory of her cuffed up or the thought of their taboo kiss, the reality is she probably can't wait to be long gone from here, home safe and sound, and have this, and him, be nothing more than a memory.

Deciding that he needs to change the subject, Adam asks her how her day went with his buddy and what they got up to while he was gone. Demi gives him a laugh and asks him if he's jealous, and he feels that old familiar twinge in his stomach, a feeling he could do without getting used to. He's also sick of hearing that word. It's a word he's used himself many times that day. "Oh, please," Adam replies, trying to play it off, "Don't be ridiculous, a day with my buddy probably consisted of a lot of fart jokes and other 16-year-old immature behavior. What could I possibly be jealous about there?"

Demi cracks up at this, long and hard. He's confused by her laughter, but the sad truth is, he isn't far off with his predictions, and once she's had herself a good laugh, she lets him know it. "Oh, I don't know, that plus a lot of boob and butt jokes seem worthy of being jealous over," she says, wiping away a few tears of laughter. "Honestly, I have spent pretty much the entire day right here on this couch. We watched some TV together and played way too many board games and card games. We were going to go outside a few times, but he kept getting distracted by phone calls, though obviously none were my mother."

She doesn't have to say that last part, but she still feels the need to anyway; every time the older guy left her and went into the kitchen she had felt her heart race in anticipation that he may be in there making phone calls about her mother. At one point, he had even said as much to her. She had felt her hopes raise every time, though she told herself it was stupid, and so far, she had only proven herself right. She has a pretty good idea that the younger one isn't as involved behind the scenes as the older one is, and so for the rest of the evening, until the phone rings or until the older one comes back from wherever it is he is, she's probably playing the waiting game just as much as he is. Waiting on her mother. Waiting to be rescued.

Adam is not surprised to learn that Brandon hadn't gone outside with Demi as he said he was going to. His friend has a way of getting sidetracked very easily, especially when it comes to money or business, and Adam can see him leaving the poor girl alone in here for an hour or even more at a time while he sits in the other room lost on his phone, planning and scheming. Adam finds himself feeling bad for her; he realizes that at this point she's been cooped up in that tiny living room bedroom area for going on 2 full days now, and she hasn't had any fresh air or much room at all in which to stretch her legs. And that just isn't being very hospitable.

A thought pops into his head, and he almost dismisses it, but then decides to go for it. He takes a deep breath, suddenly feeling nervous about what he's about to say, but he takes another deep breath and says it anyway. Feeling nervous around her is stupid. "Well, I know the sun is going to set soon, but it's still light enough out right now for a little bit longer, would you like to go for a walk out back with me? So, you can get some fresh air and stretch your legs a bit?" It comes out sounding so awkward and high school like, almost as if he's asking her to the prom, and he blushes, his embarrassment growing. He's quick to add, "But don't forget, I'm armed, and I'll cuff you to me just to be safe, so you can't run away." He's talking fast, not thinking about what he's saying or where this conversation seems to be going, and he hasn't realized how naughty that sounds until the words have come out of his mouth. This isn't helping his blush, and she laughs nervously.

Demi thinks it over. She can't lie, she's desperate for some fresh air and would love to actually walk around outside and move more than 2 feet at a time. However, the thought of being handcuffed to him is making her heart race, her breathing speed up and her palms sweat. It feels like there is a whole cage of butterflies inside of her. This is going to be some real close time together.

She knows she isn't going to be taking off in the woods in the dark, especially not knowing where the hell they are, however can she blame him for thinking that way, considering the situation? She is someone they've kidnapped, after all. And it's not like the thought of running away *hasn't* crossed her mind. For some reason, the thought that she's been kidnapped takes her by surprise, which then surprises her even more. With the older one, it's so easy and comfortable here, but it's also always business and professional, and she never once forgets that she has been kidnapped. But the moment she is alone with the younger one, everything changes, and she can lose herself so easily. At the end of it all though, she really just wants to get outside, even for a few minutes, so she takes a deep breath, steadying herself and faking a little bit of confidence, and then stands up and wiggles her wrists at him. "So then cuff me and take me outside," she says, "I'm ready."

Demi's personality continues to impress him, and surprise him, and scare him all at once. He smiles at her and then they stand up and get dressed; he throws a sweater on and lends her his jacket, and then he cuffs them together and then leads her through the house and outside. Adam is careful to walk them through the carport and then down the driveway and to the right, into the wooded area, as opposed to around the immediate back of the house. This way he is able to avoid his truck. He doesn't know why but he feels the need to keep her from seeing it parked around back.

They spend about 45 minutes outside, just walking around, enjoying the fresh air, and sharing small talk about their lives, families, schooling, interests, and friends. They are both somewhat shocked at how easy and natural the conversation feels between them once the stress and awkwardness is gone. There are a few times while they are walking when their fingers and knuckles brush, and it sends sparks through them both. It doesn't bring up the same sexual tension and anxiety as before though; out here, with the conversation flowing and the atmosphere totally different, it almost feels normal.

Once it begins to get too dark outside to see, Adam leads them back to the house. Demi's a little bummed that her outdoor trip is over and she's going inside again, but overall, she feels fantastic about having had the chance to get some fresh air and to stretch her legs, and Adam can see that happiness written all over her face.

A short while later, with the two of them back in the living room again and locked in, Adam takes the handcuffs off of her and they settle in back on opposite couches. He watches her lightly rub the spot on her wrist where the cuff had been, and it gives him an odd sense of dominance over her. For some reason, he'd love to rub and kiss that spot himself, giving her some relief, and instead finds himself telling her how thankful he is that she hadn't given him any issues. "With this being my first kidnapping and all, I appreciated the cooperation." He winks at her and says it trying to make a joke, but he isn't expecting the snappy reply she has for him. "What can I say, I'm just weak and helpless, and didn't want to put up too much of a fight this time," and she gives him a sly smile and a wink back. Adam laughs and asks her if she would like a drink, and then he gets them a couple cans of pop from the mini fridge.

When his back is turned towards her, Demi can't help but think of two things. One, he has a killer ass and looks great from behind, but that isn't her main concern. He's more like distracting eye candy. The second thought that flashes through her mind goes hand in hand with the thoughts she had the other night before she got carried away with herself. If there was some way she can get into his pocket and get the keys out of it, maybe she *can* make a run for it. Maybe she can rescue herself after all.

The plan may be stupid, but now that she's been outside, a plot begins to form in her mind anyway. They are literally in the middle of nowhere, and she knows that. When they were outside she heard no cars or traffic, and as it grew darker out, no nearby lights lit up. From what she can see, they are in a heavily wooded and secluded area. Probably 10 or 15 minutes outside of the city. And if she plays her cards right, all she really has to do is get outside. From there, there's a million places for her to hide and lots of room to run; if she sticks close to the driveway eventually she will make her way to the road, and from there she only has to flag down a car. And hope like hell the car isn't carrying her kidnappers coming looking for her.

Adam brings the cans of pop back and takes a seat on the couch opposite her, placing her can on the coffee table in front of her. It takes her a moment to register that the drink is there, and that doesn't go unnoticed by Adam. He can see how distracted by her thoughts she is. He wonders what's got her lost in her mind; if it's her mother, or if it's this situation, or maybe she's thinking about him. Goodness knows by now he's always thinking about her. What keeps surprising him though is not everything he's thinking about is sexual. He really enjoyed their time outside together and talking comfortably; once the tension's gone between them he can't seem to get enough of her and loves getting to know her better. He wonders what the rest of the evening, and the rest of the week will bring, if it ends up dragging on that long.

While Adam is fantasizing, the thoughts that are running though Demi's head are very conflicting. The more she thinks about getting the key and getting out, the easier and crazier it sounds. In reality, all she needs a few minutes to keep his attention occupied. However, tricking him like that, using him sexually, makes her feel yucky inside. Regardless of what the situation may be, she really does like him, and doesn't want to break his trust or hurt him. She just can't think of any other way to distract a guy while getting into the pockets of his pants though.

The fact that she's confused by all of this is where her problem lies. Everything about this kidnapping is weird and uncertain and out of her control. The last thing she wants is to be a victim of Stockholm syndrome, falling in love with her captor. She thinks to herself, next she'll be daydreaming about him telling her mother to keep the money, he just wants to keep her daughter, that will be good enough for him. She almost snorts out loud, but that's when her voice of reason chimes in. Yeah, and what about the other guy? What happens when he wants his money? What a joke.

The truth is, once she'd seen the keys and the thought began to form in her mind, she knew she was done for. She's tired of waiting around for her mother to save her. She's going to save herself and get away from all of this. It's time to see this crazy plan through, but how?

The tension that's slowly arising in the room again is killing Adam, and he refuses to let whatever is happening in her head ruin the good atmosphere that they finally have going on. There's still a little over four more hours before Brandon is due back from his shift, and that's a long time to sit in an uncomfortable silence together.

"Would you like anything to eat? I can go make us something?" He asks her, bringing her out of her thoughts, but she just shakes her head no. She knows her stomach is in knots, she will never be able to get food down. Besides, her mind is made up, and she's going to do this now, before the older guy comes back from wherever he is, and before she chickens out and loses her nerve. It's crazy and it's stupid yes, but she's about to do it anyway. Screw her mother. "Do you want to play some cards?" She asks him, and he agrees quickly, eager to do something a little more intimate with her than not talking while they just watch TV.

Seeing her opportunity, she gets up and walks over to the couch he's on and sits down beside him, taking him by surprise with her boldness. They leave the movie still playing in the background, and Adam picks up the deck of cards from beside the remote and begins to shuffle, asking her what she would like to play. "Totally up to you." she says to him with a shy smile and a shrug. "You pick." There is something about her attitude and her behavior that's off to him, she seems different all of a sudden, but he can't quite figure it out. He also can't figure out why her sudden change of behavior has given him a half chub in his pants.

To humor her and break up the mood again, he deals them both out a handful of cards, picks his up and looks at them, and then asks her if she has any 4's. It takes her by surprise and gets her laughing to realize that they're playing such a childish game, and for a moment she almost decides not to go through with her plan. He can be cute, and caring, and he makes her knees go weak. Regardless of what's happening, part of her doesn't want to do this. She knows it's going to make him hate her.

The thought almost ruins her mood, but she keeps with it, knowing once this is over it shouldn't matter whether he likes her *or* hates her. They get through two rounds of go fish rather quickly before moving on to crazy eights, neither of them seeming to want to truly focus on cards. Crazy Eights only lasts a few rounds as well before the tension is too much, and conversation is almost at a null. When Adam asks her if she'd like to play another round, or play something else, she says no to both, and so they put the cards away and just sit and watch TV for a while. The change is killing Adam, he doesn't know what happened after he tried so hard to fix things and they were going so well, but he needs to do something. Besides, it doesn't seem like a bad tension, it feels strangely sexual again, and he doesn't understand where that came from.

He doesn't ask if she wants another drink, he just gets up and walks to the mini fridge and grabs a couple cans of pop and sits back down beside her. There needs to be a change of pace, and he feels like he needs to take charge somehow. He keeps trying to think of something to say to her, yet everything sounds stupid in his head, and so he keeps stopping himself before he starts. So much for taking charge of the situation, he mocks himself in his head. He notices, however, now that he's come back from the fridge she's sitting a lot closer to him on the couch, their knees are almost brushing, and he can't help but wonder what's going on. His penis is also wondering, he feels himself grow a little bit harder in his pants at the possibility of *anything* happening between them again, as much as he knows he shouldn't want it to.

Demi feels like she might throw up. Her stomach is so tight in knots she can barely breathe, and her hands are balled into sweaty fists on her knees. She's so torn between doing this and not doing this, she wants to back out, but he's so close to her now; she can smell his skin, the scent of his cologne and the shampoo he used in the shower today, and she can remember the taste of his lips from last night, the pressure of his against hers, the feeling of his tongue. She can't resist. The next time that he turns to her to say something, and his face is right next to hers, she doesn't think about it she just leans closer into him.

Their lips press together for a second before either of them really registers what's happening. She knows what she's doing, but she's terrified to be doing it, and so she can barely act past initializing the kiss. That split second is all it takes for Adam to realize what's happening though, and in a moment, he's on her, kissing her back urgently, kissing her deeply, desperate for her. He reaches up to cup her face and pulls her closer to him still.

Once he begins to kiss her back she loses any reservations she has. Her tongue pushes its way past his lips, caressing his tongue, and the inside of his mouth, and her hands are in his hair and on his neck, tugging at him, pulling him into her. Her body is on fire for him, she feels like a virgin again, and she can tell by his breathing and urgency that he has to feel similar feelings. It's taboo and wrong, they know they shouldn't be doing this, and yet it just feels so right.

His touch electrifies her, and she can't wait for more. She needs to feel him everywhere. She starts to initiate everything, wanting him badly, no longer caring about her original plans and stealing the key being the furthest thing from her mind. Once his mouth is on her, and his hands are on her body, all she can think about is touching him, tasting him, and quenching this fire he's started within her.

She grabs at the bottom of his shirt and tugs on it, pulling it lose, and then her hands are sliding up underneath it, grabbing all over his chest, rubbing against him, and he moans into her mouth. He's so surprised and turned on by her eagerness for him. Her hands are so soft, so small, and he finds himself feeling harder than ever thinking about her rubbing them up and down his shaft. The thought makes him moan again, louder this time, and now he's doing the same to her, reaching up under her shirt and cupping her soft and supple breasts, surprised to feel she isn't wearing a bra. There's nothing restricting him now, especially because she doesn't try to stop him, and he pinches her nipples and rolls them between his thumb and fingers. It's her turn to moan against him, loudly, breaking their kiss to breathe heavily and lick and kiss along his neck, nibbling on his ear lobe.

Demi isn't the only one who's skin is on fire; her hands all over his hot body are driving Adam crazy. His boxers are wet with pre-cum, and he isn't thinking about anything at this point other than tasting her, touching her, and being inside of her. He just wants to pin her down and take her. Even though Brandon won't be back for a few more hours, Adam wouldn't have noticed if he was due to be back in 5 minutes. He would have kept going anyway. Nothing is in his focus at this point except Demi's hot tight body and her very wet pussy.

He isn't letting her take charge anymore, that's just not his style, and so he grabs her shirt and rips it up over her head, leaving her topless and exposing her to him. He takes her by the waist and pulls her against his body, beginning to kiss and lick and nibble on her breasts. He sucks one of her nipples into his mouth and hears her gasp and moan above him, her fingers digging into his shoulders, her thighs wrapping around his hips. He can feel the heat radiating from between her legs, and she's pretty much climbing up into his lap; sitting against his rock-hard cock, grinding on him as she pushes her chest into his mouth. He cups and rubs her other boob, tweaking that nipple between his fingers as he bites on the other one gently, and she cries out against him, making his cock twitch into her.

He can't take any more of this teasing, her moans and little cries are driving him insane, and if she keeps dry humping him like this he's apt to cum in his pants. He grabs her tighter by the hips and flips them both over on the couch so that she's laying down and he's now between her legs, pinning her with his weight. Then he leans down and kisses her deeply again, grabbing her by the hair and pulling her close. He presses his cock against her, grinding into her hard.

Demi is lost to him now, all the thoughts she had of getting the keys or escaping her captors and rescuing herself are long gone under his touch. She's only thinking about one thing right now; the guy whose name she doesn't know, who's between her legs and about to make her cum. Her hands are all over his back, pulling him even closer to her, desperate to feel him. Her eagerness is all the invitation he needs to push this further, she seems to want him just as badly as he wants her.

He slides his hand down across her tight stomach and feels her take a deep breath in, feeling nervous, sexual energy and sparks flying as he undoes her pants and slides them open. His fingers reach in and pull her panties to the side and slide along her very wet lips, lightly, teasingly. She's moaning loudly now, grabbing at him, and moves her hips upwards against his hand. He spreads her lips wide open, exposing her, and rubs against her hard clit with his thumb, making her cry out and cling to him. Adam takes one of her nipples into his mouth and bites lightly as he rubs her little nub harder, and then slowly slides his fingers down and pushes two gently inside of her, starting to finger fuck her. Demi throws her head back in ecstasy and then runs her hands down his chest, sliding them down under the waist band of his pants, eager to make him feel the same way she does, wanting to see what he's got for her.

Adam's feeling so tight and constricted in his jeans, he just wants to be pressed up against her, feeling her wetness and her heat. He gently removes his hand and pulls away from her even though she moans in frustration and protest, and she almost reaches out for him. He gets up and strips his pants and boxers off, and then he grabs her pants and panties and does the same thing to her in one quick motion, leaving them both naked. He looks her up and down, taking in her gorgeous body, and she feels her stomach tighten and heart flip flop at the look in his eyes, and the thrill of being nude and exposed for him. Then he's on her again, spreading her legs, touching her everywhere, hands all over her body, wanting to taste her and tease her and make her cum hard against him.

He can't even decide where to begin, everywhere about her is so tempting, so he starts kissing her first, pushing his tongue inside her mouth deeply while his hands explore her again and make their way down her body and between her legs.

He isn't the only one who wants to explore though, and now that he's naked nothing is stopping her from touching him too. He tries to focus on her but her soft warm hands are all over his chest and back and making their way down, around his waist and then across his pelvis. Then she's got his cock in one of her soft small hands, and she uses the other to cup the head of it. He moans into her mouth, loudly, and it makes her smile as she starts to stroke him slowly. It's nice to know she does have a little bit of power over him.

Adam starts to lose some of his concentration, feeling her stroking him in time with his fingers inside of her. He's got two of them in her again, while he rubs her clit with his thumb in time with her movements. Both of them are lost in what they're experiencing, kissing deeply, imagining more than their hands and fingers on and in each other, enjoying this incredible foreplay. "Oh my god you're so wet," he moans against her as he starts to feel her juices drip down his hand, and instead of a reply he feels her thumb slide over the head of his dick, playing with the pre-cum that's building up there, and he gasps out loud. It seems she isn't the only one who's wet.

He wants her so badly, he just wants to be buried inside of her, but he's so close to cumming already and he can't stop himself. He doesn't want to, either. It just feels incredible, and so right, and so wrong, and so exciting, and so taboo. He picks up speed with his fingers, pushing them deeper and harder inside of her while rubbing her clit in circles, and her breathing begins to speed up even more as she thrusts herself against him. "I'm going to, ugh, fuck, I'm going to cum, make me cum, please, please!" she starts to cry out and beg him, and her fist tightens around his cock as she begins to stroke him faster and faster.

She is not going to be the only one cumming. His breathing picks up too, and he feels his balls clench up, and he leans into her and kisses her. Her wet pussy starts to tighten and constrict around his fingers as she cums. Her pussy walls pulsing pushes him off the edge, imagining his fingers being his cock buried inside of her, and it twitches in her hand as he unloads hot cum all over her stomach and part of his chest.

Fuck, he thinks to himself, that was way out of line, and not classy or even respectable, and over far sooner than he liked, but he regrets nothing. It felt amazing. Demi is torn too, laying there breathing heavily underneath him, pinned to the couch, in shock by what had just happened. She hadn't imagined anything like this. Kissing, maybe even a little heavy petting, but not this. Whatever happened to making out, so she could grab the keys? None of this was part of her plan.

Adam looks at her, and the mess that covers them, and lets out an awkward laugh. "Um, yeah. I'm going to have to get us some toilet paper or something and get this cleaned up." She laughs nervously too, suddenly consumed by everything all at once, overwhelmed and tired and so emotional she almost wants to cry. Short and unexpected as it was, that had been an incredible and amazing sexual experience, and her body is screaming out for more. She's still light headed and breathing heavily from one heck of an orgasm, finally one that she hasn't had to give to herself. And now suddenly this is the moment that she's done all of this for, and she's hesitant and scared to take it. She's so torn and conflicted by her feelings that she doesn't know if she's actually going to be able to go through with this. She has to admit, she likes him, and it's screwing everything up.

She watches him get up slowly from the couch, trying not to make an even bigger mess, and he heads for the bathroom. Sitting right there on the floor in front of her are his pants, and the pocket that contains the keys to her freedom. His gun is also sitting there, attached to the belt holster, but she doesn't give it a second thought. She isn't going to shoot him, and so she doesn't even think about taking it as a threat.

Demi takes a deep breath and forces her mind to stop screaming and tries to steady herself. She's stark naked right now, but if she grabs her shirt and jeans on the fly, she can get them on outside in the dark. Probably. She just needs to be able to cover herself, forget the rest. She doesn't need to be picked up naked, that certainly won't help her mother's reputation now would it? She takes one more deep breath, telling herself she can do this, that she's brave enough, that he's probably only fooled around with her because she's a girl and girls are easy, and besides, she had been the one to come onto him anyway. That thought gives her a burst of anger at herself for liking him in the first place. To finish it off, she reminds herself that doing this means she's free from her mother having to save her, she'll be able to rescue herself.

And then just as Adam turns and shuts the bathroom door, she reaches down quietly, snatches the keys and her shirt and jeans, and makes a silent run for the door.

Chapter Thirteen:
Monday Evening

Demi's palms are so sweaty she almost drops the keys out of frustration and nervousness. Her legs are wet from her juices, and her chest is sticky from his cum. She feels disgusting and thinks to herself that this has to be by far one of the stupidest things she's ever done in her whole life. She should still be laying there naked on the couch instead, waiting for him to bring them toilet paper so they can clean up, relax and enjoy the moment, whatever the moment was.

Instead, she gets the living room door open and then almost forgets the keys in the lock before remembering that the guys are smart, and the outside door is locked too. She's trying to be quiet, but she's desperate to get out now that she's so close to freedom. She grabs the keys and takes off down the hall, terrified, not bothering to shut the door behind her. He's going to know she's gone anyway, so why waste any extra time.

Adam shuts the bathroom door for only a moment; he has to take a leak something awful, and he'd rather not do it in front of her. He grabs the toilet paper roll right off the holder when he's done and starts wiping up his chest when the thought occurs to him that he's not wearing his jeans, and the keys and gun are still on the waist band. Shit, he thinks, how stupid can he be? He throws the door of the bathroom open, heart racing, telling himself that he's being ridiculous, no girl would ever be that ballsy, but in his heart, he knows that's just not true, not about this girl. She's already shown herself so different, she's got spunk, and personality, and *she's not in the living room!!*

He slams his fist into the wall beside him, not hard enough to punch a hole but just hard enough to let out a little frustration. Stupid, he is so stupid. Brandon is going to kill him. He sees the living room door left wide open in his mad dash to grab his jeans. What takes him by surprise is that she hasn't taken his gun, just the keys, and some of her clothes by the looks of it, though she left her panties. He could almost laugh at this if things were different.

He can hear the keys jingling in the kitchen as she fumbles with the kitchen door; she hasn't even gotten out of the house yet. He takes the extra second and throws his boxers and jeans on, doing them up on the run down the hall just as he hears the kitchen door slam open. She isn't going to get far now.

Demi struggles more with the kitchen door than anything. Her heart is racing and the blood in her veins is pounding, she's terrified of what's going to happen when this guy catches up to her. She's just gotten to the kitchen when she hears a yell and what sounds like a bang from the living room behind her; he's come out and found her gone, and she needs to hurry her ass up. Her hands are shaking so badly she can barely get the door handle to turn and open, and once she does the cold air hits her naked body and the reality of what she's done truly sinks in. Here she is, about to run off into the cold, in a forest, in the middle of nowhere in the dark, while naked and covered in cum. What the hell is she thinking?

Which is exactly what Adam yells to her in anger as he comes running down the hallway and into the kitchen after her. Upon hearing his voice, she panics and leaps down the steps, making it about 6 or 7 feet out into the driveway before Adam is behind her, grabbing her. His strong arms surround her, and then she's pulled back against him, his hot chest and rough jeans digging into her skin, reminding her that she's stark naked. His breath is hot in her ear, and he sounds angry, and hurt. "Are you *serious*?? What the HELL Demi!" He yells at her and slides an arm under her legs and lifts her up off her feet in one swift motion. She opens her mouth to yell out or make some comeback or scream, but his other arm is suddenly around her shoulders and his hand clamps down tightly on her mouth. He's holding her terribly awkwardly, but tightly against him, and she feels his heart beating wildly in his chest as he stares down at her with disbelief and anger and a little bit of sadness in his eyes. The truth is, she has no idea what she was thinking, and she feels just as bewildered as he does.

She could probably try to squirm out of his grasp or grab or claw at his hand or body with her free hand, but she already knows she's beat, she knew it from the start. This was a really dumb plan. Regardless, he doesn't trust that she won't try to make a break for it again, and he shifts the way he's holding her and throws her up over his shoulder fireman style. She drops her clothes accidentally, startled by the movements and totally shocked and embarrassed to be suddenly so exposed. The thought of the way her body's open right now doesn't skip past Adam either, and he feels himself growing semi hard again as he squats down and picks up her clothes and then heads back towards the house with her. She is in the perfect position to administer one hell of a spanking, he finds himself thinking.

He kicks the door all the way open, and it bangs against the wall and stays there as he leaves it open and makes his way through the house with her. He kicks the living room door open and then the small bedroom next, depositing her roughly on the cot. He turns to her and finally unholsters his gun, and then waves it at her. Demi may not have been ballsy enough to take the gun in her haste, or to use it on him, but he clearly had no issues threatening *her* with it, and he's certainly done playing games.

She takes a deep breath, feeling scared, suddenly realizing just how much deep shit her actions may have got her in. Keeping the gun aimed at her, Adam throws her shirt and jeans at her and then walks out into the living room backwards, never taking his eyes or his gun off of her. He bends down and scoops up her panties and then the cuffs off the table, and then walks back into the bedroom. "Get dressed, now." He says to her, full of attitude and totally in charge. She swallows hard against the knot in her throat, knowing how badly she screwed up. She dresses quickly, a little embarrassed to have him staring at her while she dresses, but then again, a few minutes ago she had let him strip her naked and have his way with her.

When she's finished, he points the gun at the cot and tells her to sit down. Again, she does as she's told, feeling very submissive to him, and humiliated at the same time. And it's all by her own doing. In one long stride he's at the side of the cot with cuffs in his hand, and he cuffs her one arm to the side of the cot and walks out with his back to her without saying a word or even shutting the door. Demi stifles a sob, trying to be quiet, but she can't stop a hot tear from sliding down the side of her face.

Adam is pissed. Beyond pissed. He cannot believe what's just happened in the past hour, and he needs to get everything back together, fast, including his head, before Brandon returns and finds out anything went wrong. All the evidence has to be covered up. His heart is still pounding in his chest, and he's breathing heavily. His hands are shaking, and he can't quite think straight. He feels like a teenager whose parents are about to come home and bust them for getting up to no good. And he feels like such a useless *tool*! He let his guard down and screwed everything up over a girl and his fucking penis, just like he always does. What if she had somehow managed to get away, and *that's* what Brandon was coming back to instead? What if all of this had gone very, very, differently?

Adam went and let himself get used for something, what else is new. Sex, money, freedom from him, it was all the same. She didn't want him. She hadn't wanted him at all. All she wanted was a chance to grab the keys and make a getaway. That doesn't explain why she hadn't taken the gun, and actually gotten away with her plans, and it also doesn't explain her passion and urgency for him, and her wetness, but that was beside the point right now.

He gets up, heads out of the living room and makes his way down the hallway and straight back out of the house again, examining the driveway and the carport and everything around him. It doesn't look like there's been a struggle or anything out of the ordinary, but he is absolutely not taking any chances right now. He's only got about an hour or less until Brandon comes back and he wants to get things as normal looking as he can.

He wanders back into the kitchen and finds the keys still dangling out of the open kitchen door. Of course, why would she take them, if she didn't need them after this? He knew it was a good idea not to let her see his truck parked around back. He pulls the keys out of the lock, shuts the kitchen door and locks it behind him. He has a quick glance around the kitchen and then makes his way back down the hallway, locking the living room door behind him too.

He looks around the living room, avoids looking at her doorway and sighs heavily, and then walks over to the mini fridge and takes a beer out. He makes his way back to the couch, sits down and cracks his beer open, still not looking at her, not speaking to her, not even acknowledging her. He needs a few more minutes to try and get his head together before he can trust himself to open his mouth. He's dumbfounded over what an idiot he's been about her. But he doesn't want to yell at her, or scare her, or snap on her either. He's better than that. So, he sits calmly and drinks his beer, waiting for Brandon.

Demi watches Adam come back into the living room and get himself settled on the couch. He's sitting with his side to her and his face is turned away; not looking at anything in particular except maybe the wall. He seems tense and miserable and she can't really blame him. In her mind, somehow, she had only seen them making out a little bit, and when he was distracted she'd sneak the keys from his pocket, and then she'd just wait until he was in the washroom and then make her grand escape. In her head it sounded easy, and dumb.

Just like the guys and the kidnapping, she had never planned for anything to go wrong, or even to get carried away and lead him on like that, she had never planned for anything too sexual to happen between them and she never meant to hurt him or make him angry. But she's surprised to find herself feeling angry too. He does something crazy to her and it makes her act out in carnal ways. He makes her crave dirty, naughty, awful acts she hasn't realized she even wanted from deep down inside of her. She wants to be helpless at his control, wants him to tie her up, use her, tease her, make her beg for more, make her beg for him to let her cum, make her beg for him to stop. And all of that mixed with her desperate need to run away and free herself from her mother has screwed everything up. She doesn't feel like she should be entirely to blame here.

And she doesn't even truly understand where the idea to grab the keys had come from in the first place. She IS in the middle of nowhere, and she's being held captive by guys with GUNS. What the hell was she thinking trying to run away, and naked at that? To prove something, to who, herself? That she doesn't need her mother to save her? To prove that she can rescue herself?

These thoughts make her suddenly sit up right in the bed, even more pissed with herself, using her free hand to wipe away her tears. All this time in therapy and she doesn't even realize that the whole escape plan was a subconscious way of saving herself before her mother could. To prove she doesn't need her, just like her mother obviously doesn't need *her*. The rest, well, what can she say about the sex part? If she was honest with herself about that too, if she had met him somewhere else, and began dating him, and talked to him about her wants and desires in the bedroom, she highly doubted he'd mind one bit taking her over his knee and spanking her. For the first time in her life she'd felt accepted by someone for a brief moment, and all those things had collided to make a big mess of everything.

Chapter Fourteen:
Monday Night, before midnight

As the silence drags on and the night continues, the tension between them grows. Demi is desperate to say something, anything, just to make him look at her, to remove the cuffs and let her apologize, but she knows any of that would be useless, so she sits in the silence. Adam too, would love to say something, but he keeps his mouth shut for other reasons. He has nothing nice to say to her right now and he knows that if he starts to say anything, everything is going to come out in a flood, and Brandon will be back soon. He needs to calm himself before that, he doesn't need Brandon returning to the two of them in some sort of lover's quarrel.

As the time passes, Demi begins to feel really uncomfortable. Between the stickiness of his cum still dried all over her chest, causing her shirt to cling to her, her own cum that's dried all over her thighs, and the need to pee, she doesn't know how much longer she can sit there for. She's fidgeting on the bed, trying to gather up the nerve to call out to him, but as she opens up her mouth to finally say something to him, she shuts it, remembering that she still doesn't know his name. Here she is, torn between going gaga over this guy and threatening her life trying to run away from him, and she doesn't even know what his name is. She could almost laugh. Does she just yell out hey handsome? Or hey kidnapper? Instead she clears her throat softly and calls out, "uh, hey?" Her face flush in embarrassment at even speaking. But when she sees his shoulders tense at the sound of her voice and she gets no reply from him, she feels the embarrassment turn to heartbreak really fast, and another tear falls down her face.

Thankfully, it isn't long before Brandon returns from work.

He walks into the kitchen, puts a few things away that he bought after his shift, and then heads down the hall to the living room and lets himself in. He enters to find the atmosphere as tense as it's been yet, he feels like he could cut through the thickness of it with a knife. Adam's sitting on the couch, drinking a beer, and he barely nods at Brandon's arrival. There's evidence that Demi's been out here at some point; cans of pop are lined up in both spots and the cards are out, but she's not in the living room. Instead, he finds her sitting on the cot in the small bedroom, and she waves a cuffed hand at him in greeting and looks away sheepishly.

Brandon looks back at Adam in disbelief and raises his eyebrows at him questioningly, but Adam only shrugs back in return. "Do I even want to ask what's been going on here?" Brandon asks, but he's not even sure he wants an answer by the way Adam rolls his eyes and takes a swig of his beer first. "I don't know man, why don't you ask her?" And Adam nods towards the small bedroom door.

Brandon looks at Demi for an answer, and at first, she can't give one at all, she can't even think past the thought that Adam didn't rat her out. He didn't make up a story to cover his side of it, didn't tell his buddy anything, he just left it all to her. He could have told his buddy everything and made things very difficult. But if he isn't going to tell on her, then she isn't about to either. So, she follows suit, shrugs and says she doesn't know, then gives the older guy a half ass smile, hoping that some sexy charm will rub off and maybe, crazy thought, they can all just pretend this never happened.

Brandon looks at her long and hard for a moment, thinking, and then he turns back to Adam. "Well it hurts my heart to see a pretty girl all cuffed up like this, so I'm going in there to take them off of her, so she can have something to eat and get settled for a bit before bed. I don't even want to know how long she's been in there for." He turns back to Demi, and unholsters his gun. "And just in case you thought I was, you know, too soft, I'm not nearly as easily persuaded by a sexy body as my partner here is, but, you're always welcome to try." Brandon laughs at his own corny joke, and then wanders into the bedroom to remove the handcuffs from her.

She avoids making eye contact with Brandon when he comes in the room, feeling embarrassed that he's finding her like this, even if he doesn't know what's going on. She's terrified that he'll take one look at her and read it all over her face. Once she's free, she mumbles thank you to him and makes her way out to the washroom without making eye contact with Adam either, staring at the floor the whole time. Well, this is going to be a long night, she thinks to herself.

Demi takes a few minutes to give herself a bit of a wipe off in the sink, and glances at the shower in the corner while she does so. She's sure if she asks the older one when he's there alone with her tomorrow, he'll let her have a quick shower. That is, *if* she's there alone with him, what if her foiled escape plan tonight ruins things? She really hopes it's just the two of them in the morning, as she could sure go without the tension when the younger one's around... but then again, being alone with the older one in the morning likely means being alone with the younger one in the evening again, and after tonight, she's rather scared about how that's going to play out.

If her mother doesn't get the message and call sooner, she'll be coming home on Thursday as she plans this time, which means Demi has still got two more days here, and that may very well mean two more evenings alone with the younger one. She swallows hard against the lump that's forming in her throat, knowing she needs to get herself together and go back out there. She wishes so very badly that she had a time machine; she would go back in time *right now* and take back all of her behavior in this, from the horny thoughts and the scene in the bedroom, to their shared kiss, to the incident from not long ago. If only none of this was her fault.

When Demi comes out of the bathroom a few minutes later the guys are seating on opposite couches eating some late-night snack foods. She feels like she has to choose between a sleeping snake and an angry one, so she takes a seat on the couch beside the older one, feeling like he is the lesser of two evils right now. The tension in the room is obvious to all of them, and they're sick and tired of it for their own reasons.

Demi's still thinking about a time machine and how much she regrets her involvement in things. She knows it does her no good to be caught up in this mental cycle, but her mind goes around and around in circles just adding to her funk, and she doesn't even look at Adam at all and can barely glance at Brandon when he speaks to her either. She picks at her food, not feeling that hungry with her stomach tied up in knots, even though she really only ate a late lunch and then skipped dinner in the midst of their crazy sexual adventure and then her ruined run away.

Adam tries to tell himself that he's pissed off at her, and a little piece of him actually is, but for the most part he's just hurt. Really, really hurt by her. And it kills him inside, because he simply hadn't been expecting it. He's spent the last little while trying to convince himself that this has been a part of some plan she's had since the moment she realized she'd been kidnapped, and that's the only reason anything happened between them at all.

Part of his mind is screaming at him, arguing with him that her passion, her heat, her dripping wetness and her very, very, real orgasm say otherwise, and didn't he instigate some of that himself? But he pushes the thoughts aside. Right now, it's not even that he's convinced himself that she used him just like all the other females in his life either, it's that he's hurt. He feels stupid to admit that he was actually starting to like her, and he let his guard down.

And as for Brandon, well on top of the fact that the kidnapping is still dragging on, he's just sick and tired of this high school crush stress and tension those two have going on between them. He doesn't totally understand it, but it's beginning to affect everything and he's so ready for it to be over. Their sexual need for each other is driving him absolutely crazy.

After another twenty or so agonizing minutes of silently watching TV, with no one having been willing to say anything to break the quiet, Brandon gets up and orders her to start getting prepped for bed. It's earlier than last night, but no one is going to complain or argue the fact. Demi is feeling exhausted and has been trying not to yawn for some time now. Between that, the tension, and all of her emotions, she is ready to be alone for a while and just shut down.

She grabs some clothes from the small room and takes them into the washroom with her. She brushes her teeth and washes her face and then slowly gets herself changed and ready for bed. When she comes out of the bathroom, she sees that the younger one hasn't even moved from the couch, and he's still facing the TV, clearly lost in his head, keeping his gaze away from her. The pull out hasn't been made and no one else is ready to call it a night.

Demi isn't about to press her luck tonight, the older one is standing by the doorway to her bedroom and he's got his hand on his hip just beside his gun holster. She feels sad at catching herself referring to it as being her bedroom. It's only been two days, but those two days have certainly felt like a lifetime. She goes in without a fuss, and he hands her a water bottle just like last night. But unlike last night, the younger one isn't awaiting in her line of sight as the door closes, looking at her with those big blue bedroom eyes, and this time she isn't upset about it. Her stomach is in turmoil and she just wants to lay down and relax.

The door shuts on her, the locks click into place, and she just stands there for a moment, staring at it, lost, before she lets herself fall back onto the cot. Suddenly everything crashes down on her all at once. All the embarrassments of the day, and the stupidity and humiliation, all the sexual adventure and lust, all the things she wishes she could do over or take back begin to overwhelm her. She tries to settle her breathing and her heart rate, knowing that's about the only thing she can control right now, but even that's hard for her. She still can't figure out what has made her behave this way, acting out on these cravings the younger one brings out from inside of her.

Demi hears the living room door shut and then total silence surrounds her. There are no sounds of the TV, or the pull out or couches squeaking, not even any sounds of shuffling or whispered talking. She figures they've gone into the kitchen to talk, or even left the house all together. It doesn't really matter to her or affect her at this point, so she pushes the thought out of her mind. She's emotional and exhausted and she just wants to cry, and so she lets herself do just that. Demi curls up into a ball, hugging the blankets against her tightly as she rolls over onto her side, and sobs herself quietly to sleep.

Even with Demi gone to bed, the tension doesn't fully subside like Brandon assumed it would, which tells him that a lot of the anxiety is actually coming from Adam. The thought gives him an enormous amount of stress. He nods for them to go down the hallway into the kitchen, and Adam follows him, locking the living room door behind him, knowing he's about to get scolded like some horny teenager once again, what else is new. He also knows he totally deserves it, but the problem is, he just doesn't want to crack or have Brandon find out what really happened here tonight.

The guys get to the kitchen and Brandon grabs them a couple of beers from the main fridge and joins Adam at the kitchen table. No one says anything for a few moments, they just take the time to relax and enjoy their beer in silence. Adam finds once he's out of the living room and away from her presence, and the scene of the crime so to speak, his whole attitude seems to change. He hates what she's doing to him.

"Listen man," Brandon says, interrupting Adam's train of thought. "I've said it before and I'll say it again now. I'm not going to ask for all of the details, the less I know, the better, but I'm not dealing with some petty high school shit just because you're looking to get your dick wet. There are plenty of girls out there who would *love* to give you the time of day, and you know it. So maybe tomorrow you should go and utilize that a little bit and give us all a break before you blow this. Because you are *not* going to blow this for us. I won't allow it." Adam doesn't reply to this, he just sits quietly and picks at his can, thinking about everything they've talked about. He knows Brandon is right, but he also knows that until this is all over with, he's not going to be able to get that sneaky bitch out of his head.

After a little while of sitting there in silence, Brandon realizes that Adam isn't going to say anything back to him. That's fine, but he isn't dealing with it anymore. He gets up and finishes off his beer and places the can on the counter. "Alright," Brandon says, "I'm off to bed. You can lock up behind you when you're done and ready." He gives Adams shoulder a tap when he walks by, and then he's gone, leaving Adam alone with his thoughts.

However, his thoughts and being alone in his head isn't a place even Adam wants to be for very long, torturing himself with what ifs and whys. He's got so many questions he doesn't have answers for, and so much anger and hurt inside of him. He quickly finishes off his beer and follows in his buddy's footsteps a few minutes later.

He gets back to the living room to find it dark and quiet; the bathroom door is open with the light off, Demi is locked in her closet room, and Brandon's bedroom door is half shut. Adam's the only one left up now. He uses the washroom and unfolds out the couch, and then lies down with his thoughts for a very restless and anxious sleep, turned with his head facing her doorway.

Chapter Fifteen:
Tuesday Morning

Demi wakes up feeling like she's been hit with a sack of bricks. It's as if she's been out all-night drinking and dancing, and now her whole body is sore and has one awful hang over. She'd had a terrible sleep and woke many times throughout the night from bad dreams and been unable to get back to sleep right away. She figures she probably rolled around restlessly more than she actually slept last night.

She takes a deep breath and lets it out slowly, reminding herself that she only has two more days of this, and she can do it. She's strong. After this is over she never ever has to see these guys again, and she can move on with her life. The thought gives her both relief, and sadness. She curls back up into a ball under the blankets and waits for morning.

It isn't much later that someone comes to her door and knocks softly, and then she hears the lock turn. She tells herself that she's being completely ridiculous, but her stomach fills with butterflies in hopes that it may be the younger one waking her up. Maybe they can talk about last night and make everything alright again. It's wishful thinking, but she can't stop herself from thinking it anyway.

Demi gets out of bed and stretches slowly, feeling her body pop and crack and ache in protest at such little exercise lately. She walks to the door and opens it to the aroma of good strong coffee. She breathes it in, grateful for the smell this morning, and sees the older guy sitting on the couch pouring himself a mug. The pullout has been tucked away, and there is no sign of his friend. She is dying to ask where he is, if he's OK, if he's mad at her, but she keeps her mouth shut and smiles back at Brandon when he raises a mug at her. She doesn't want to give away anything from last night. Demi uses the washroom, and then walks over and takes a seat on the couch opposite the older one.

Brandon eyes her up as she makes her own mug of coffee and takes a big sip, watching her savor it. She looks rough, and he's not entirely sure whether that's just because of the kidnapping and the last few days wearing on her, or if it's Adam, and whatever is going on between the two of them. He also notices her hair is a stringy mess that she's got pulled up in a bun on the top of her head and guesses she would probably love to shower. He imagines he'd be feeling pretty nasty right about now himself. He's been fortunate enough to be able to shower at work before his shift, and Adam has been showering at his own apartment.

He waits until she's had a chance to enjoy her coffee and wake up a bit, and then he asks her if she'd like to shower today. The look of absolute gratitude on her face makes him smile, and the smile lets some of the tension he's picked up this morning slide away.

"Yes, please!" She says, practically shouting at him. "I really wanted to ask you guys if I could have one today, but I wasn't sure if you or your buddy would let me, and I didn't want to push my luck." He gives her a laugh. "Well, we can't have you sitting around here stinking the place up, now can we?" She pretends to be insulted, and mocks sniffing herself and makes a stinky face, and Brandon lets out another big laugh. The girl has a sense of humor, and she has been a sport about the whole situation, he will give her that much. He's enjoying being in her company when it's just the two of them.

Once they've finished their pot of coffee, Brandon gets her a towel from the closet in the bathroom and lets her take a shower. He tells her that the time doesn't matter, so she takes him on his word and stays under the shower stream until the water turns cold. Demi scrubs at herself furiously until she feels as clean and free of the last few days as she can be. She takes a little longer than she needs to get dressed and braid her hair over to the side, but she wants to feel like herself again, as much as she can.

When she comes out of the bathroom and sits down on the couch, Brandon sees her and almost has to do a double take. Even with no makeup on and obviously just the bare essentials she's had to work with, she's still done a great job making herself look nice. He can see why Adam would be taken with her; she's a natural beauty and a firecracker underneath that soft shell.

Brandon eyes up her appearance again and a thought crosses his mind; he hopes she hasn't dolled herself up like this for Adam. He sees this thought as an opening to talk to her about what's been on his mind concerning her and his buddy. "Hey, I want to talk to you about my friend," he says to her gently once she's sitting down again. Demi looks at him in anticipation, terrified that somehow, he found out what happened last night; either the other guy finally ratted on her, or she's about to get in shit for something regardless. Despite his gentle tone, there is something else underneath it.

Brandon sees her guilty look, and it adds to his confusion, but he lets it go. "I know something's been going on." He holds up a hand to stop her from interrupting him or saying anything. "Now, I don't know exactly what, so you can wipe that look off of your face, but I'm also not an idiot, and I know my friend well. You two had a moment of some sorts. Probably a couple of them. Maybe you kissed, maybe more, or maybe not." She feels herself start to blush at this but forces herself to focus on what he's saying. She doesn't want to give herself away.

"He hasn't talked to me about it, but he doesn't have to. He's all sorts of messed up when it comes to women, he always has been, and probably always will be. And that leads me to my point here. Even if we *weren't* in this situation together, and I just happened to be his roommate, or his friend and we were having this conversation, I would still tell you to steer clear of him, and to smack him if he comes on to you. He's trouble. But we *aren't* having this conversation under other circumstances. For the next two days, we *are* your kidnappers, and this tension, this sexual chemistry, it's killing everything. I'm the boss here alright? So, I'm asking, no, I'm telling you, for the sake of your sanity and myself and the whole atmosphere we have going on, please, try to cut the flirty shit out OK? Or at the very least, don't make it any worse. Alright?"

She snorts, but she doesn't really answer at first, thinking over what he's said to her. She can't say she hasn't been the reason behind some of the tension and sexual happenings, a lot of this does fall on her, so she needs to admit to herself that she does carry some of the blame. She takes a deep breath. "Alright," she says finally, almost rolling her eyes, feeling a little embarrassed and a little like she's being scolded by a parent. He gives her a hard look, debates telling her how serious he is, and then decides to change the subject instead. "So, are you hungry for breakfast yet?"

Demi's stomach rumbles loudly at the mention of breakfast. It turns out she's starving. He leaves her for a bit to make breakfast, locking her in the living room once again, and she passes the time watching TV, wondering if her mother will ever get the damn message and call for her, wondering what beach she's currently soaking it up on, or what country she's backpacking through, and what next man she's bedding. She shakes her head, annoyed with all of these dumb thoughts of her mother flying through her brain. She has made up her mind; after all of this is done, she is taking a long overdue vacation, and never coming back to her mother's house again. It's time to move on.

Chapter Sixteen:
Tuesday Afternoon

Once Demi's had a chance to scarf down some breakfast and settle her stomach, the rest of the morning and afternoon pass rather enjoyably for her. Since Brandon's said his peace, he feels much more at ease with her, and she has never felt much tension with him anyways. She's showered and changed and has to admit that after a couple more mugs of coffee, she's starting to feel human again.

The two of them watch a movie together, play some board games, and take a long, handcuffed walk around the property. She is extremely grateful that he has a chance to take her outside today. While they're out there, Demi sees that in the light, this place really does seem like it's in the middle of the forest in the middle of nowhere; they walk for quite some time in a few different directions and never see anything but trees. She's reminded once again about how much of an idiot she'd been the night before; for all she knows she could have died out here in the cold, she could have fallen and broken something, and she would have been running around totally lost and stark naked in the dark. Once that scene begins playing through her head again, she's reminded just how awkward tonight is likely going to be.

When they come back inside, he lets her get settled in the living room and then Brandon heads into the kitchen to make them some soup to eat for lunch. All in all, Demi is feeling wonderful, it had been lovely to be outside with him, and she feels even more refreshed. There isn't any weird sexual tension between Demi and Brandon while they're cuffed together, or when they spend any time alone together for that matter, they're just very relaxed and comfortable with each other.

After lunch they play a few hands of cards and watch some more TV. He starts to glance at his watch an awful lot, and she can feel the tension building as he grows more and more anxious as the clock ticks. Demi is actually relieved to know for once it doesn't involve her, and she doubts it has anything to do with the ghost phone either. She has a feeling that the older one is going to work every night while they take shifts watching her, and he's probably going to be late if he's keeping the same schedule every day.

That may be a lot of assuming on her part, but yesterday the younger one had come back fresh like he'd just recently had a shower, and seemed awfully relaxed, while the older guy seems to be on a tight schedule and tends to come back tired like he's just worked for hours. So, like Brandon had done earlier, she uses this opportunity when the thought pops into her head to ask him that very thing, if they're taking shifts while also working. Brandon gives her a nervous laugh and tells her that if it was any of her business, she would know, and she takes that as a yes.

That thought is confirmed a little while later when Brandon is practically pacing the living room and debating whether he can get away with leaving her alone and locking her in so that he can leave, when they hear a door slam open further in the house. Then there's an awful lot of banging, and they hear Adam stumbling loudly in the hallway. He fumbles for a bit with the lock and then throws open the living room door too and almost bumps into Brandon as he's trying desperately to get his bearings and shut the door again behind him, reeking of alcohol and clearly half in the bag.

Seeing Adam like this totally surprises and appalls Brandon and catches him off guard for a moment. He is not leaving her alone with Adam like this without talking to him first. With a look at Demi he grabs Adam by the shoulder and half pulls him and half drags him back out into the hallway, shutting and locking the living room door behind them.

Demi watches the door shut and hears the sounds of them shuffling down the hallway, out of earshot. She doesn't dare get up off of the couch to go to the door and try to listen, as much as the suspense is killing her, she knows better than to press her luck now. Besides, she'll likely find out what's going on soon enough anyway. She sits tight and forces herself to concentrate on the TV, and not about what's to come; being left alone for the next ten hours with the younger one half drunk and already in a mood.

Brandon drags Adam down the hallway and into the kitchen and throws his ass into one of the chairs at the table. Adam doesn't say anything, he doesn't need to. He hadn't intended to get drunk. He had gone to the liquor store on the way to his house, thinking he'd have a shower and then have a drink or two just to take the edge off. From there, Adam had planned to go out for a bit. He was going to take a walk, hike down to the water front, anywhere. Just to be outside in the fresh air and mentally escape.

Instead, he had sat in his apartment and drank himself stupid thinking about Demi and everything that had happened between them. From there he had got sick and lost track of time, and knew he was never going to make it back here before Brandon had to go to work. Adam had then paid a cab some damn good money to drive him out here in a rush, being in no shape to drive himself, and he knew he was going to get chewed out for that too once Brandon either questioned his driving abilities or noticed his truck wasn't parked around back like it should be. Good job on not leaving any trails, he mentally chides himself.

Brandon gives him an awfully dirty look, and then goes and gets him some water from the fridge. He waits until Adam's had a good drink of it before he starts to talk. "This isn't acceptable. I'm about to call in sick to work today if you don't get yourself together, NOW. You need to promise me you won't be drinking anymore. Not at all. Not a drop. You get drinking and you start losing your self-control. Promise me you'll only have water from here on in."

Adam scoffs at this, although he knows he's right. Alcohol is not his friend. If it was, he wouldn't be here in this awkward situation in the first place. "Fine." He says back, though he doesn't look up from his glass of water, fidgeting with it between his hands instead. But Brandon isn't done yet. "You know, I may be going out on a limb here, and I don't know what the reason is for you guys having this ridiculous tension going on, but she's a good girl, and I don't think she meant any harm by whatever her part in it was." Adam raises his eyebrows to this and starts to cut Brandon off, but Brandon raises his hand up at him for silence and continues.

"I don't think you actually realize the kind of charm and flirty behavior you put off towards women. All women. All the time. And I get it, I do. You do it, probably even subconsciously, because even though you SAY you don't want to be with a woman and don't love them, you do. You put it out there desperately man, and I bet deep inside you're just a sensitive softy looking for one of them to really love you back." Brandon says the end of this with a laugh, trying to ease some of the tension he knows is sitting there, building up between them. The guys need to keep the peace between themselves above all else.

Adam is speechless. The guy who always seems to have a snappy comeback for everything, truly doesn't know what to say right now. He's never looked at his love life or himself quite like this before, and he's a little thrown off by his friend's honesty, but he thinks Brandon's right, even though it kills him to admit it. He's also not so quick to speak because he feels a little scolded, like his father caught him up to no good again and now he's getting a lecture about it.

Adam opens his mouth once more, still unsure what he's even going to say for himself, or if he can trust himself to talk right now at all, and instead he just lets out a good long sigh, feeling depleted. "I will get myself together." Adam says at last. "I just need a few more minutes before I go in there. I promise. And only water, scouts honor."

Brandon slowly eyes him up and down one last time, checking him out, seeing if Adam looks like he's sobered up at all. He thinks about calling in to work again, but after running all the scenarios through his head, he decides not to. Instead he bids Adam goodbye and leaves, locking the kitchen door behind him. He's out of sick days and he has already taken all the extra time off he can leading up to this. *If* anything goes wrong, and he hates that word, he refuses to leave any trails of suspicious behavior behind him.

Adam watches Brandon leave, and he takes a few deep breaths, staring at the closed door, willing himself to sober up just a little bit more. He finishes up his bottle of water and places it on the counter, stalling for just a few more minutes. When he's ready, he walks down the hallway and lets himself into the living room, locking the door up behind him.

He finds Demi sitting on the couch that he usually sleeps on, and she's watching TV. She looks up when he walks in, and then looks away quickly, not keeping eye contact. He feels a bit embarrassed for his entrance earlier, and his face grows red. He tries to hide it by walking over to the fridge to get something to drink. He doesn't need anything, but he needs the distraction; he isn't ready to deal with her yet and he's dreading the interaction. He opens the fridge and looks at the cans of beer. He sighs and curses himself inside his head, and instead of the beers, he grabs two cans of pop.

Shutting the fridge, he walks over to where she's sitting and hands one to her. "Uh," he says awkwardly, clearing his throat, "I'm, um, I'm really sorry about earlier. And I'm sorry about my behavior the other night. Although, you did kind of deserve it, all things considering." He gives her a little laugh at this to show he doesn't mean any hard feelings and smiles at her slyly, and then he sits down on the other couch across from her. That may have been awkward, but he can admit to himself that he feels a lot better now that he's at least apologized to her.

"Um, thanks." she says, and takes the can from him, feeling equally as awkward with the situation. They sit in silence for a few minutes and watch TV, and thankfully the tension isn't as high as it usually is between them, though Demi knows that with the silence it will get there eventually. She wants to apologize too, there's a lot of things that she's dying to say to him, but all of those things could open up a can of worms, and she doesn't know if that's a good idea or not with everything on egg shells between them, one-minute OK, the next minute tense.

Demi feels like her head is about to explode. It's barely been a half an hour since the older one left, and there is no way she can go the entire night under all this pressure. Especially because she knows a night of awkward tension is worse than saying what she has to say.

"I'm sorry!" She blurts out, loudly, and then automatically feels stupid and laughs nervously. And then she opens her mouth and the words and feelings she's been holding in all come flooding out. "I mean, I'm sorry too for last night. I never really meant for any of that to actually happen, I don't even know what I was thinking. Well, I mean when you guys first brought me here I'll admit I saw the keys and you were cute and I just, lying in bed when I was cuffed up I made up this stupid fantasy, but it was more sexual than anything. Obviously." Demi feels her face flush at the memory, remembering all too well the scene he had walked in on.

"Anyways," she says, trying to move on quickly, her words coming out faster and faster. "Last night, I didn't really plan that. I had thought about it, and then all of a sudden it was happening, and it was so hot, and it was not what I imagined would happen at all." She swallows hard, not looking at him, feeling embarrassed, and also feeling her stomach tighten as she grows horny remembering the night prior.

"And then," she says, continuing to ramble, "After we were done, the keys were just *there*. Right there in front of me, asking me to go forward with my plan, saving myself so I didn't have to wait for my mother to rescue me. I hate that she gets to save me you know. It kills me. So, I just panicked. I knew it was stupid the whole time, that it wasn't going to work, that you were going to catch me and that I was just making a mess of everything. And I was naked. Jesus. I can't believe myself. I'm sorry." She feels herself blush here and trails off.

Adam sits quietly for a minute, eyes on the TV, holding his can of pop in his hands but not moving. He's thinking about everything she's just said and feeling a little overwhelmed by her little bout of honesty too. It seems to be "let's all be honest with Adam day", but he appreciates it a lot. Her honesty is something he isn't expecting, and so he decides that it's his turn to give a little honesty back to someone.

"Well, I guess that sort of puts everything on us both you know. I didn't exactly get into this thinking *anything* that's happened was going to happen, hell I didn't even know what you looked like until we grabbed you. I don't really think highly of women or have a lot of trust for them either. I've been feeling a lot of stress over this whole situation, because I have a bad tendency to fuck up when it comes to women, and I really felt hurt thinking you planned all of that on purpose. I didn't know how to handle feeling hurt, which only made me angry. Which caused me to get drunk this afternoon. Way too drunk." He pauses, and almost leaves it at that, but then finishes his thought sadly under his breath, "Because women always have a habit of running out on me after anyway." He laughs at his last comment, to try to shrug off some of the emotion that goes with it, but Demi doesn't laugh along with him.

Instead she finds herself feeling for him, a lot, and what comes out as a reply is "Well, it isn't exactly like I ran out while we were cuddling after sex like normal couples would." She doesn't quite mean it the way it comes out, she only wants to let him know that running away from *him* wasn't her sole intention, but it still ends up sounding very emotional. She laughs nervously, trying to break the tension, and he smiles back at her, and a lot of the stress leaves the room. They both lean back into the couches that they're sitting on and watch TV in silence, but it's a comfortable silence now, each of them lost in their own thoughts related to what she had mentioned, and what it would be like if they had met under different circumstances, and things were different between them.

After a little bit of time passes, Adam feels his stomach rumble and realizes that he hasn't had much more than a liquid diet all day. Demi hears it and lets out a chuckle. "Well, on that note," he says, "Would you like me to go make us up something to eat? I know I could certainly use some dinner." Demi agrees, feeling like her appetite has grown tremendously now that things are much more relaxed between them, and Adam lists her off a few things he knows he can make for them to eat for a late supper.

When they've both agreed on something they want, Adam leaves her in the living room and locks the door behind him and heads off to the kitchen to cook. While he's gone, Demi gives herself permission to let her guard down for a few minutes and relax. It has felt great to let all that off her chest and for them to be talking and feeling good again, even if it's good in the weirdest way. The tension between them has really been the worst part of all, it's been harder on her than the actual kidnapping. Knowing she may get through tonight alright makes her breathe a lot easier.

A short time later Adam comes back into the living room with a tray of finger foods and deep-fried snacks and takes a seat beside her on the couch, depositing the tray in front of them on the coffee table. It seemed weird not to take a seat across from her, but he's enjoying the intimacy they're sharing.

There's no small talk as they eat supper, but that's OK, as the silence is comfortable, and they're both starving and ready to eat. However, during their meal, they begin to drift closer to each other, and within a few minutes their knees are touching, just a light brush. The tension starts to grow again as they finish off dinner, but it's not a bad or awkward tension, it's that same sexual tension that's been underlying everything since the beginning. Demi is surprised she can eat with her stomach all tangled in knots, she's surprised she's not on the verge of being sick having him so close to her.

They finish eating, and time continues to pass as they keep watching TV, avoiding talking to each other. They are lost in their heads, thinking thoughts they know they shouldn't be, and they both know that talking too much is only going to lead to trouble. But the sexual chemistry continues to grow between them and life can be funny sometimes. A few minutes later, a scene comes on the TV where two people are kissing heavily and groping each other.

Suddenly, it's as if a switch has been flicked on in the room, and the mood goes from tense to sexual overload. It's almost unbearable. Scenes from the last few days are still playing out in both of their heads, but mostly they are thinking about what had happened between them the night before, and how hot it had been.

It's almost too awkward for them to be sitting beside each other watching this movie anymore. He almost wants to change the channel, but then again, he doesn't want to interrupt anything that's going on between them either. If something is going to happen, he's willing to let it. Adam clears his throat, Demi shuffles around a little bit, and as they continue to fidget beside one another it becomes clear how extremely uncomfortable they are both getting. Adam can't get over how passionately she kissed him the other night, and how wet she had been. And how desperately she had clung to him while she came. It's killing him to know for sure if she really does want him as badly as he wants her, without the keys or her freedom being the reason.

Adam just can't take it anymore. Between the sexual tension that's growing and growing and the question that's burning on his mind, he feels like his head might explode.

They have a few more hours before Brandon is due back for work and he's never going to make it if this keeps up. He takes a deep breath, feeling scared about what he's about to say, and then he just says it, opening his mouth and letting the words come out, nervous stutter and all. He doesn't want to feel how he's feeling anymore. "So, that uh, that passion between us yesterday, um, you weren't faking that, just for the key? You, um, you really wanted me?" He needs to know to settle the pain in his heart, he needs to know she wasn't totally using him, and he doesn't even care that the question comes out like a teenager, asking if his crush has a crush on him too.

"I don't know what came over me," she replies, keeping with the honest trend. She's embarrassed by her feelings too, but she doesn't want to hide anything. "Like I said before, it all happened so fast, too fast, I wasn't ready! It was like all at once my stupid fantasy was coming true. But then, nothing else went as I had planned in my head." She pauses for a minute, and then continues. "And no, I didn't fake all that other stuff." Demi feels herself blush at the thought of how wet she had been the night before, soaking his hand and the couch below her. "It was just really different for me; this whole experience has been hot, and taboo and it just did something to me that I hadn't expected." She lets the last few words all come out in a rush, feeling embarrassed and a little taken back at continuing on with this honesty kick she's on. She glances towards him to see if he's looking at her, or if he has anything to say, or to add, and when she does, she finds his face right there beside her.

Adam can't help himself any longer. Everything she's saying is turning him on and making him crazy inside. If she really did want him as badly as she had shown him last night, even if it was in the moment, he has to have her again. He has to feel that passion and *craving* again. He isn't thinking straight any longer and doesn't want to. He doesn't want to second guess himself or stop this, he just wants to taste her again, touch her again, and finally be inside of her.

When she turns towards him, he just leans in. He doesn't tell himself any bullshit or lies or talk himself out of it. He already knows that what he's doing is wrong and taboo, he knows it's only going to make everything worse, and for all he knows Brandon could come back early and bust them, and then he'll *really* be fucked, but he doesn't care. All he cares about is being with her, right now in this moment, and the heat between them.

He leans closer and hears and almost feels her suck her breath in hard in anticipation, and then their lips are touching. Softly this time, gentle, exploring, tasting, yet desperately needing. His tongue makes its way past her lips and into her mouth. His kiss takes her breath away, but not her need, and she's quick to kiss him back, pressing her tongue against his just as urgently. She feels him moan into her mouth, and she grows wet at the sound of his enjoyment. Their heat is intense, and the passion is high, yet neither of them are in any hurry to rush things, not after last time. Not when they don't know what the future holds.

They spend a few minutes locked in a slow sensual embrace, sucking on each other's lips, licking and nibbling on each other's neck, hands in each other's hair, pulling themselves closer into one another. Demi can't get enough of him; his touch sends sparks through her that end right between her legs. By the time he makes his way down there she's going to be soaked right through her jeans.

Adam is eager to be between her legs too. He's so desperate for her, and after yesterday it's all he can do to keep himself from ripping all of their clothes off and taking her right here and now on the couch, ending it in an instant. He doesn't want to admit it, but he knows that this may be their one and only time together, and he plans to make the most of it. He's also feeling smart enough not to let her take advantage of him again this time. He will be in charge and take control. And he's going to be in control of every inch of her body too.

He grabs her by the back of the neck while kissing her, his fingers entwined in her hair, and lowers her to the couch. Then he slides up between her legs, using his knee to force them apart. He grabs both of her wrists in one of his hands, and he raises them above her head and pins them there, continuing to kiss her, pushing his tongue deep into her mouth. She moans loudly at his display of dominance over her as he restrains her, and she thrusts her hips up into him, her body crying out for contact. Her pussy is soaked already, and she needs to feel his cock inside of her. She's so turned on by him taking over, she has no desire to fight him, and simply lays there allowing him to do whatever he wants with her, giving herself up to him.

Adam starts by pulling away from her mouth slowly, breaking the kiss by sucking her lip between his lips for a moment, lingering there, licking lightly before releasing it. Demi moans and lifts up against him. Then he takes his free hand and pulls her shirt up over her chest and head, leaving it around her arms, pinning her with it, and exposing her breasts to him. Her nipples are already hard in excitement, and she loves feeling so vulnerable, exposed and unable to do anything about it. Adam takes his time, pinching one of her nipples gently while sucking on the other, rolling his tongue around it in circles, pulling it into his mouth. Her hips are still jammed up against him, and his hard cock is pressing tightly against his jeans, fitting nicely into her groove. He can feel the heat of her, and he thrusts back a little, teasing her, loving the sound of the little moans that escape her.

He kisses his way over to her other nipple, giving it some attention too, and then he licks and gently bites the sensitive skin on her breasts and along the underneath of them, then down around her rib cage, making her jump and giggle, pushing and squirming against him even more.

Teasing her is only teasing him too, he's so hard it hurts, and his boxers are tight and uncomfortable, soaked in his pre-cum. He needs more of her. All of her. He needs to taste her.

He reaches down and undoes her pants, and then he grabs the waist band and pushes them down to her knees. Demi throws her hips up to help him so fast he almost laughs at her eagerness. "Good girl," he says to her, causing her to bite her lower lip. Once he's got her pants down near her knees he leaves them there, keeping her legs and knees pinned and her thighs pressed tightly against the ache between them. Demi is now only covered by her panties, and pinned down helplessly, and she knows they won't be long to follow, leaving her naked and putty in his hands.

He sits up for a moment, his hands still pinning her down, and he admires the view; her hot tight body is wiggling underneath him, eager for his touch. Their eyes meet, and his stomach tightens and his cock throbs in his pants. He runs both of his hands from her shoulders all the way up her arms to her wrists, holds them up above her head, and kisses her deeply, laying against her, rubbing his cock on her through his jeans. She moans into his mouth, and her body shudders under him. Breaking the kiss, he licks his way along to her ear and tells her very sternly, "Keep being a good girl for me. Do not move your hands."

Her stomach's in knots and her body is trembling. He's doing all the things she wants done to her, and she is helpless for him right now. She does as she's told and doesn't move her arms an inch as he kisses and nibbles his way back down her body. He didn't say anything about the rest of her body though, and she's withering underneath him, moaning and whimpering. He gets to the waist band of her underwear and licks along the elastic line, teasing her, listening to her draw in a sharp breath and push up higher against him. He holds her hips down firmly with one hand and with the other, he slowly pulls her panties to the side, exposing her. He breathes on her gently, his warm breath surprisingly cool, and he loves the sounds of whimpers and moans that come from her.

With his free hand Adam reaches for her, touching her lips gently and spreading her folds apart. Demi bites her lip in anticipation, feeling so vulnerable. Her smell is intoxicating to him, and he can already see, and feel, how wet she is. Adam can't wait any longer for her. He leans forward and licks her from her hole to her clit, tasting her, hearing her cry out when he lightly circles her hard nub. He flicks it with his tongue and sucks on it softly, and then slides two of his fingers deep inside of her tight hole. They glide in so easy as she's already soaking wet.

Demi's hands are balled into tight fists over the arm of the couch, her fingernails biting into her palms. She wants so badly to touch him, to feel him, to run her fingers through his hair and push him into her, but she doesn't dare go against what he said. She wants to please him this time. So, she groans and lays there and lets him take her, however he wants.

He can't get enough of her, burying his face into her pussy, covering himself in her juices. She's moaning and pushing against him and he can hear her breathing speeding up and her whimpering get louder. If Brandon came home, he would hear them from in the driveway, but Adam doesn't care about anything anymore, nothing matters right now except making her cum, and then making her cum again, and maybe again. He quickens the pace of his fingers inside of her, pushing into her deeply, while sucking on her clit and rubbing it with his lips and tongue, and whispering for her to cum for him. His words vibrate against her sensitive areas. It isn't going to take her long now, and she lets him know, begging for him as he speeds up even more and adds the odd nibble to her clit and lips, driving her crazy.

Demi can feel the rush taking over her. She loves that she's not getting off on some fantasy in her mind, she's not forcing anything, or faking anything, and she's not pretending he's some other person or that she's in some other scenario either. She's lost in the moment as it's happening, lost to the feeling of his fingers inside of her, and his tongue all over her, and the tightening inside of her. She loves the thrill of imagining being tied up and vulnerable and helpless for him, and she especially loves the thought of pulling against her restraints and fighting against him, forcing him to hold her down and take her, claiming her, making her all his. Almost punishing her for the last time. She loves how he's taken control of her, dominating her, and she totally lets herself go, moaning that she's cumming for him. Her pussy starts to pulse against his fingers and he feels a rush of juices coat him as her thighs tighten against his hand, pinning his fingers into her, holding him close. He keeps licking her and pushing his fingers in and out, letting her come down from her orgasm, enjoying every last drop of her.

As her breathing slowly begins to return to normal and her body relaxes under his, he pulls away from her slightly and uses the hand pinning her hips to lift himself up. He stares into her eyes as he slowly undoes his pants and slides both his jeans and his boxers down to his knees, letting his cock spring free, watching her reaction. Demi bites her lip again in anticipation, thinking about having him filling her, knowing it's only moments away.

He grips one of her legs firmly around the thigh and slides her leg free from her pants and pushes them over to her other leg, out of the way, freeing her. Then he slowly makes his way back up her body, kissing her, touching her, pinning her, pressing himself against her, and finally spreading her legs apart, totally opening her up to him. His hand moves from holding her hips down to back up to her wrists and he grabs her again, tightly, taking back control. He kisses her deeply, pushing his tongue into her mouth, and she can taste herself on him. She feels the heat of his cock pressed up against her wet slit and she grinds against him, and he moans against her lips in return.

Adam can't take it anymore. All of this teasing is driving him wild. He has to bury himself inside of her tight wet folds, now. While he's still kissing her, he reaches between them with his free hand and grabs his cock around the base. Pulling his hips back a bit, he rubs the head in circles around her little bud and then down around her open slit, wetting himself, watching her squirm under him like jello. Teasing them both just a little bit longer, even though he's almost mad with the urge for her.

He has a brief thought of her all tied up on a bed, really tied up with soft ropes, spread open in front of him, fully exposed, letting him really have his way with her. The thought makes him moan aloud, and in one smooth thrust he buries himself inside of her as far in as he can go, so deep his pelvic bone rubs her clit, and she cries out and thrusts her body up against him. She is so tight and so wet, clamping down around him, just like he knew she would be. He knows it's not going to take him long to cum.

He uses his weight to pin her down into the couch beneath him and grinds his hips into hers, moving his cock around slowly inside of her. He lays his face down by her neck, kissing and nibbling on the sensitive skin there, and then licks his way up along the lobe of her ear. She's pulling against his hands, trying to free herself, to touch him, to feel him, he's driving her crazy and she's desperate for him. He's never had this much control over a woman before, and he loves the thrill of having her helpless and putty at the touch of his fingertips.

He grabs the ankle he's already pulled free of her jeans and brings her leg up to her shoulders. This lets him get as deep in her as he can go, and he feels the pressure of her tight hole engulfing him as he pushes against her cervix, all the way in. Demi cries out loudly, and pushes back against him, matching his thrusts and his eagerness. Then Adam's lips are covering hers, and his tongue is just as deep inside of her mouth. Sparks are flying between them, their chemistry is through the roof, and they can both feel that an orgasm is about to overtake them. He picks up his speed, really taking her now, fucking her roughly, needing her, needing to take her, dominate her, control her, own her body, fill her with him.

They're both hot and soaked in sweat, and their skin sticks together when it touches. They're on fire for each other. He lets go of her wrists and she's on him in an instant, grabbing him around his back and pulling him closer to her, clinging to him, her nails digging into him. She whispers into his ear that she's cumming for him again, and that pushes him over the edge; Adam feels his cock twitch deep inside of her as her pussy walls tighten and clench around him, milking him. They cum together, moaning loudly, grabbing at each other desperately. He thrusts into her a few more times, catching his breath, feeling the last few pulses of her wetness surrounding him and then he leans in and kisses her one more time before he pulls away.

Adam doesn't want to think about anything other than right now here in this moment. He doesn't want to think about what just happened, or what the future holds. He glances down at their entwined bodies and he knows that they're both a mess, but he isn't an idiot and isn't taking any chances this time around. He hadn't even fully undressed himself, he's still got his pants around his knees and his belt on with his gun and keys attached.

"I'm going to grab us some toilet paper to clean up." He says to her, pulling away and standing up. "Between the gun and keys, which I *still* have on me this time, I'm hoping there won't be any issues, but just so you know, I have no troubles cuffing you up again." He winks at her, and she blushes, and despite the fact that she's very much pleased and exhausted, she feels herself grow wet once more at the thought of actually being cuffed up and at his disposal again, just like she had been imagining. She pulls her shirt down and sits back on the couch, waiting for him. She doesn't want to think past this moment either. She just wants to relax in it and enjoy it.

Adam comes back with a roll of toilet paper and they take a few minutes to clean themselves up and use the washroom, but neither of them talks much. There is so much uncertainty now, and far too many unanswered questions, and if they don't talk, then none of that has to be talked about. He grabs all of their garbage and tosses it in the can beside the mini fridge, then he gets them both a couple of beers. He knows he promised Brandon that he wouldn't drink, but he only wants one, and at this point, he really needs one. He sobered up pretty quickly once things had begun to happen between the two of them, and besides, how much worse could the night get?

After they've both had a chance to get settled and dressed and put themselves back together, he takes a seat on the couch beside her and hands her a beer. She thanks him, and opens it, and they sit back and watch TV, not touching, and not talking. They are both filled with so many questions, wondering what they each want, wondering what they want from each other, what the other one wants, and wondering why things are happening the way they are. But neither of them breaks the silence, and slowly the tension begins to build again, only this time it isn't sexual, it's just uncomfortable and awkward.

Brandon gets back to the farm house from work part way through the movie they are watching, and he couldn't have come in at a better time. At that point, Demi has her empty can of beer in her hand, playing with it, fidgeting with it, unable to stay still, and Adam keeps opening his mouth and shutting it again, so unsure of what to say, terrified to talk, not wanting to know the answers, and yet wanting to say and ask everything all at once.

As Brandon walks in the living room with a few late night fast food snacks in a bag in his hand and shuts and locks the door behind him, he's glad to see that the atmosphere isn't at its usual tense peek, although it isn't super comfortable either. He's also glad to see Demi isn't locked up in the bedroom again. There's something about the two of them sitting together on the couch though, with the atmosphere feeling odd and weird, that gives him an equally odd thought. And he's not thrilled to see the beer cans. "It smells like sex in here," he says with a half laugh, and he takes a seat across from them on the other couch. It is weird to see the two of them sitting beside each other on the same couch, even if they aren't touching. Something has definitely changed.

Adam responds to Brandon with a half laugh of his own and tells him he has no idea what he's talking about, but Brandon can't help noticing that Adam's laugh sounds very awkward and slightly nervous, almost forced, and Demi turns a few more shades red and turns away. It seems like that girl is always blushing. He thinks about it, then decides he's not going to ask. He's all but begged and pleaded with these two to keep their hands off of each other, but they're two adults and clearly don't listen worth shit to anything except the calling from in their pants. Plus, Brandon thinks to himself, after tonight there's only one more night and then HOPEFULLY all of this will finally be over and done with, and he can take off to a beach somewhere and forget about it all, a million dollars richer, and neither of these two will be his problem anymore.

Brandon dumps the bags of food on the coffee table in front of them, and they dig in and eat in silence while the movie plays on in the background. If nothing else, Brandon knows he can be grateful for the slight change of pace throughout the room, with these two getting along for whatever reason, there isn't the usual "so tense you want to snap" mood surrounding them.

Regardless, Brandon is still very eager to get to bed and get this day over and done with. There's only tomorrow, just one more day after this. And then one more night. And then it will finally be Thursday. It seems like it's taken a lifetime to get here.

When the movie's over and the credits begin to roll he turns off the TV and gets them up and going through the usual bedtime routine. Demi uses the washroom first and gets herself dressed and prepped and ready, and then she makes her way to the small bedroom. She keeps her eyes on the floor, not making contact with the younger one, feeling so torn. The thought of being locked up alone in that little room tonight makes her feel really sad, and she almost resists going in, but then she doesn't. It would be stupid with the older guy here, he doesn't take any nonsense, for him this is all business, *and* he doesn't need to know what happened. He would have no problem pulling that gun out and waving it at her, forcing her into the room for the night. But oh, what she wouldn't give to curl up on the pullout couch beside the younger one and fall asleep, even if they don't talk about anything, even if they could simply cuddle to sleep, just holding each other after everything that happened.

Demi doesn't even look back when she goes into the bedroom, and as Brandon locks the door on her turned back, she doesn't even respond to him when he tells her goodnight. He turns around from the door and finds Adam sitting faced towards him, as if he was watching, waiting for her to turn around, to see her before Brandon shut the door on her. Which is weird, Brandon finds himself thinking, because Adam is always faking like he's not interested. "Yo." Brandon says, walking over to the coffee table towards Adam, and he says it with a little more anger than he intended. "I need to know I can trust that this door is going to stay locked. OK?" He asks Adam with a stern look, but he loses a bit of the gruff in his tone, and Adam nods back, looking down at the ground.

"I. Yes. I," Adam stammers for a moment, breathes deeply and calms himself, then goes on. "I know I'm an idiot, but I won't do anything to screw this up. I'm sorry." Brandon stares at him long and hard, thinking over a bunch of comments he wants to make, but everything that runs through his head sounds rude, or nasty, and Christ, he thinks to himself, this is almost over with. He needs to keep the peace. So instead he says nothing, turns and makes his way to the bathroom, and gets ready for bed. When he's done he heads into the bedroom without a word or a glance at Adam, who's been busy pulling out the couch, but he doesn't shut the bedroom door behind him. He hasn't shut the door yet, and he isn't about to start letting them have any more leeway or privacy then they've already had.

Adam waits until Brandon has gone to bed before he gets up and uses the washroom and gets ready for bed himself. Then he just sits down on the edge of the pullout, lost in his thoughts. He feels like he's never going to sleep tonight. Not after everything that's happened. He puts his hands on his hips, feeling the keys in his pocket through his jeans, and looks at her door, sighing heavily. He hears Brandon begin to snore from the bedroom, and he realizes he's been lost in thought for some time, thinking of all the things he'd love to do if he could only open that door, if only Brandon wasn't sleeping in the next room, if only things were different, and this wasn't a kidnapping, if only they were anywhere but here.

Thinking about all of these things he doesn't understand and can't change is driving him crazy and mentally exhausting him. Eventually, he lays back on the pullout with another heavy sigh and laces his fingers together and puts his hands behind his head. He doesn't even undress or lay under the covers. His eyes feel like sandpaper, yet when he closes them, he just sees her and her gorgeous naked body running through his mind. So instead, he stares at the ceiling, wondering if she's sleeping yet, what she's thinking about, what she wants from him, and what's going to happen once this is all said and done. Over time, his eyelids finally grow heavy and his mind shuts off, and he falls into a restless sleep full of questions and need and longing.

Chapter Eighteen:
Wednesday Morning

Demi has an awful sleep, and she wakes before anyone else does, laying on the cot listening to the silence of the house. This will likely be her last full day and night here before she gets to go free tomorrow, providing her mother calls. She doesn't know if the thought makes her happy or sad. Without knowing what's going on, what the future holds, without knowing if she will ever see him again after this, and not understanding what she's feeling, she's very conflicted and anxious. Her stress is enough to keep her from falling back asleep again even though it will be a few more hours before anyone else is awake.

She is not the only one up this early though. Adam has been awake most of the night, restlessly tossing and turning, lost in thought. He's angry with himself for letting everything get so out of hand, considering the situation and the circumstances that surround them. He's mad at himself for letting his guard down, because he knows now he feels a lot for her. Way more than he ever expected to feel, and way more than he knows how to deal with. He's terrified that she doesn't feel anything back for him, or even still, that maybe she does, but they won't be able to do anything about it. Hell, after this he may never even see her again.

He lets out a small sigh and rolls over on the springy pull out. The sun hasn't even rose yet and he's already exhausted with the day and everything that's going on. These have been a few of the longest and craziest days of his life and he just doesn't have it in him anymore. When this is all over, one of the first things he wants to do is sleep. Except he aches inside knowing that he may never sleep beside her, after he's finished having his way with her again, and again, and again.

There's only a hint of sunlight on the horizon and Adam is already up, having tucked the pull-out bed away prepped the living room and gotten himself ready for the day. He can't sit here all morning and he can't stand driving himself crazy thinking about the evening that's coming, either. Everything about this place, having to see her this morning, having to make small talk between the three of them, it's enough that he wants to punch something from the stress.

He doesn't even stay to make himself a cup of coffee, though he does set the machine up to start a pot for Demi and Brandon for when they get up, and then he quietly calls a cab to come and get him, as his truck is still at his apartment. He could probably drink a pot of coffee to himself as it is and doesn't want to waste any more time. He plans to grab one on the run, maybe a few of them, and then spend the day in his apartment; he needs a shower, he needs to jerk off desperately as he can't get last night out of his head, and he needs to check out for a bit and have a nap in his own bed. He hasn't been sleeping at all and barely feels human. He doesn't plan to do any drinking, not after yesterday, he just wants to be alone in the peace and quiet and familiarity of his own place and leave all of this for a while. He writes a note for Brandon and sticks it on the counter beside the coffee pot; letting him know that Adam couldn't sleep well and that he promises to be back earlier this time, totally sober, and then he's out.

He leaves quietly and waits for the cab outside. He gets the driver to drop him off at his place, and then he gets straight into his truck and drives to the nearest coffee shop and grabs himself a large take out coffee. He drives around for a while, even though his eyes feel like sandpaper and he wants to go home. He just drives. He just can't seem to grasp that tomorrow everything will change. He'll be rich, emptying out his apartment, leaving the life he knows behind and making a run for it. Starting over fresh. Starting over somewhere new where he doesn't have any debt, and no one knows his name, and no trouble follows him around. The thought should make him happy. But it only makes him sad. Because tomorrow, he'll be leaving her.

It isn't long after Adam's left that Brandon wakes up and walks out of the bedroom. On the way to the washroom, he notices the pullout is empty and put away, and it gives his heart a scare for a moment, thinking that Adam may have crept into the bedroom with Demi after all. But when he knocks on her door a few minutes later and wakes her up after he's used the bathroom, he finds her in there all alone.

Brandon can smell coffee coming from down the hall in the kitchen, and he assumes that Adam is either in the kitchen still, or he's up and gone awfully early this morning. He leaves Demi to wake up and get herself dressed, and then he locks the living room behind him and heads out to the kitchen. He finds the place empty, but he also finds Adam's note and the freshly made pot of coffee. He shakes his head while reading it; he will be so glad when this is all over tomorrow and he can be done with all of this teenager crap. He takes what he needs and places it on a tray and then makes his way back down the hallway.

There's a big change in the atmosphere in the living room today. Brandon knows something must have happened last night, but as far he can tell, it's making things a lot easier around here. He turns the TV on for them and they settle in for a lazy morning, pouring a couple of mugs of coffee and letting themselves wake up a bit.

However, nothing wakes them up quite like the sound of the ghost phone that begins to ring around 10am. Demi damn near jumps out of her skin, having almost forgotten what a ringing phone sounds like. She simply wasn't expecting it to ring. Her mother is so flaky sometimes, Demi assumed that her mother would have no idea until she got home and found the ransom note tomorrow morning.

Unlike her, Brandon has been on pins and needles ever since their first connection didn't take place, and he's spent almost every moment just waiting for the phone to ring. It's been mentally exhausting. As time ticked away he had started to lose a little bit of hope that it would happen before Thursday, but not all, and now it feels like it's all been worth it.

He hadn't totally been prepared this morning though, and the phone is in the pocket of his jeans instead of on the coffee table in its usual spot. It takes him a moment to fish the phone out, and Demi is watching him anxiously and nervously, ready to tackle him and answer the phone herself if he doesn't hurry up. Her mother is calling. She's finally calling. All of this will be over soon.

Demi holds her breath, watching his every move closely as Brandon answers the phone. And then she hears her mother's familiar high-pitched voice, screaming over the other end of the line. Suddenly she's on the verge of laughter; she can hear her mother's hysteria, and she's probably terrified, but five minutes after this is all said and done, she knows her mother won't even ask her if she's OK. And the truth is, as far as kidnappings go, she's fantastic. It's everything else that's a mess right now.

She listens to the older guy try and calm her down, and he tells her the details of the kidnapping and what she's supposed to do now. Demi hears her mother cut him off a few times, and he looks at her and rolls his eyes and makes the yap, yap, motion with his hand, and Demi has to cover her mouth, so she doesn't laugh out loud. That won't exactly help things. Her mother demands to speak to her, so Brandon hands her the phone briefly, and she lets her mother know that she's fine, and hands the phone back. Demi doesn't have much else to say to her, and she almost has to bite her tongue as it is.

Once Brandon has gone over the details of the money transaction a few times with her, and he's had her write the banking numbers down, he hangs up the phone, feeling really relieved about everything. He turns and looks at Demi. "Well, seems like you're going home early. Your mom's already at your house, she caught an earlier flight and got the note we left originally. She's sending the money, and once it checks out, you're out of here. I just need to go make some calls and get a hold of my buddy." Then Brandon gets up and leaves her in the living room without another word and locks the door behind him. It doesn't matter anyway; in the silence of his absence she has nothing to say. Her thoughts are over taking her at an alarming rate, smothering her, threatening to give her an anxiety attack.

Suddenly, everything is happening fast. Way too fast. She really thought she was going to have one more night alone with the younger one. She didn't even know what was going to happen, she just *wanted* it to happen. Even if it was awkward, and nervous, even if it was uncomfortable, and they didn't talk. What if she has to go home today and doesn't get a chance to see him again? It's still early, and he doesn't normally come back until a few hours after lunch. Will the older guy wait for him? She hates to admit it, but the thought of this ending *right now* is tearing her apart.

A half an hour later her fears are realized. Brandon comes back into the living room and tells her that he can't get a hold of his buddy, but that her mother has already sent the money through, and now it's time to go. Demi looks up at him from where she's sitting on the couch, not saying anything at first, trying to process what he said to her. It takes her a moment, and then she bursts into laughter and tears all at the same time in this great big burst of emotion, and it shocks her to the core.

"Hey, hey now," Brandon says, taken aback by her display of emotions, feeling really awkward and unsure of what he's supposed to do. Does he comfort her? Console her? Does he hug her? Are those happy tears, or sad tears? Isn't she thrilled to be going home? He can't imagine that it's Adam's absence that's making her feel this way, he assumes it's just an overload of everything that has happened to her the last few days all coming crashing down at once.

"I know you don't really have many things here, considering we took you in your pajamas, but if there's anything you want to take with you, any of the clothes we bought, whatever, please, feel free to grab it." Brandon says to her when she's had a chance to calm herself a bit. "Whatever is left will just get thrown out anyway. And then, let's hit the road, and get you home."

Demi stands up in a daze, still not talking and almost unsure of what to do first. She wanders into the small closet bedroom, and glances at the clothes on the floor. In the midst of that pile are the t-shirt and shorts that Adam lent her the first night she was here. She knows he'll likely be looking for them, but she takes them anyway, stuffing the whole bundle of clothes into the plastic bag from the store that was still in the corner as to not be suspicious. Then she wanders slowly back out of the bedroom. All that's in the bathroom are a toothbrush and some deodorant, and she doesn't need to bring those with her.

The entire time that she's packing, and slowly making her way to the living room door where Brandon awaits, and then through the house and out the kitchen door to the van, she's hoping desperately that the younger guy will come back early. She's purposely dragging her feet and taking longer than she needs to, hoping that it will just come out as her being moody and tired. Brandon echoes her feelings a few times though, once or twice muttering under his breath and a few times right to her, that he doesn't understand why his buddy isn't answering his cell phone, and why he's chose *now* of all times to totally disappear off the map.

They leave the house and Brandon locks the kitchen door behind them out of habit. Then he opens the passenger door of the van for Demi and she climbs inside, feeling numb, and lost in thought. Everything seems to be way out of her control right now, and it serves as a reminder that she never really has been in control. It's Wednesday after all, not Thursday, and she doesn't have that one last day that she thought she would. She never escaped that night, never rescued herself, she only ended up tying herself and her emotions closer and closer to her kidnapper, some regular Stockholm syndrome right here. Hell, she doesn't even know what his name is. They had shared some of the most intense and hottest sex that she's had in her life so far, sex that left her craving more and more, and then they'd never spoke after. And now she may never even speak to him or see him again, and she doesn't even know if he would want to speak to her either. Her head is a mess and she feels sick. And it's not like she'll ever ask his buddy about him, he's already given her the talk about how he feels. Thinking about the older guy makes her remember she doesn't even know his name either, and she takes a glance at him as they pull down the driveway and out onto the road, heading back towards town.

Brandon catches her looking at him and he lets out a laugh, breaking the silence and the tense mood. "I bet you're awfully glad to be going home huh? I know I sure would be. What's the first thing you're going to do? Have a hot shower? Make a home cooked meal?" "I'm going to call the cops on you two," she snaps back quickly, and the look he gives her is enough to set her into almost hysterical laughter.

"I know, I know," she says after a few minutes, wiping tears from her face, "bad joke. Sorry. But can you blame me? I'm so tired right now. What I really need is some sleep." He gives her a sideways glance, debating how joking she really is, and if maybe he should pull over or not, and then he lets it go and gives her a laugh back. "And yeah," she finishes, "I could probably use a shower too." She glances out the window after that, watching the trees pass by, and bites the inside of her cheek to focus on anything other than the emotions threatening to overwhelm her and the tears that are ready to fall.

They don't talk anymore after that. Ten minutes of driving later, Demi starts to see more and more houses and then a few stores line the side of the road as they travel towards a more populated area and get closer and closer to the city. She feels her stomach clench in anticipation and nerves. This is really over. She's really going home.

Brandon pulls into a park area that's across an intersection from the mall parking lot. "This isn't quite where you're meeting your mom, but I can see the meet up spot from here, I can probably pick her car out if I look for it, and besides, I don't want to risk being seen by any security cameras." He pauses, taking a deep breath, and Demi fidgets with the bag in her lap, causing it to make a crinkling sound in the silence of the stilled engine. "Your mom is waiting in the parking lot across the street. I told her to park in that row over there facing the other street. I should be able to see you get to her, and then I can leave with the traffic at the lights and then just drive on into the sunset." He laughs at his corny joke, but it makes Demi feel awful in the pit of her stomach. The guys have the money, and she's leaving. It's done.

She's desperate to ask him about his friend, she knows now is her one and only chance to ask him about the younger guy, and she's leaving, what does it matter? But Demi just doesn't have it in her. She can't stand to hear him tell her instead that she's better off staying away, or just leaving things alone, because she already knows that. She doesn't want an answer of disappointment, she's disappointed enough with herself.

Suddenly he's interrupting her thoughts. "But in all honesty, this has been quite the experience. A little weird, yes, and not what I expected, but I'm glad all is done with now, and it ended well for us all. And it was nice to have met you, you know. I hope you do something with your life kid," he says softly at the end, "Don't just go home and fall back into depression."

His kindness startles her, and so she does something equally as startling; she leans forward and gives him a big hug. "Thank you, for uh, for not being all the scary things you could have been. I'm not going to lie, I was really terrified when you guys grabbed me." And with that she pulls away, and they just sort of look at each other for a moment and share a laugh. Then Brandon reaches over and opens her door for her and tells her to get out.

Demi undoes her seat belt and takes the plastic bag in her hand and slowly gets out of the van, shutting the door behind her. She locks eyes with Brandon one last time, swallowing hard, knowing that this really is her only chance, and she almost cracks and asks him. She hesitates for one brief instant, and then she takes her hands off the side of the van, waves goodbye, and starts walking across the parking lot to the lights and waits for her turn to cross, refusing to turn around, and refusing to wipe away the tears streaming down her face.

Brandon watches her cross the street when the light says walk, and she heads straight for the far row of cars at the side of the lot by the other street where he's told her she'll find her mother. He starts his van as he watches her mother jump from her car and grab Demi in a big hug, similar to the one she'd just given him. He's satisfied that she's back and things are done, and so he pulls out of the park area, through the lights and back out towards the farm house.

Chapter Nineteen:
Wednesday Afternoon

Brandon checks his personal cell phone a few times on the way back to the house, even though he's not supposed to be on his phone while driving, but the anticipation is killing him. He keeps sending texts and calling, but he can't get a hold of Adam, his phone has been off all morning, and he's pissed that Adam's still pulling this moody crap. And that he got left to deal with all of the business stuff by himself. I should have taken a bigger cut, he thinks while driving back.

Adam's truck isn't in the driveway when Brandon returns, and he isn't surprised. His note may have said he won't cut it short this time, he promises, but Brandon knows his friend better than Adam probably knows himself. He's an open book most times. Adam doesn't know that Demi isn't here anymore, so he won't be so eager to spend any more time shacked up buddy, buddy with her than he has to, even though he wants to, desperately. It's written all over Adam's face every time he looks at her, every time he talks to her, every time her name is brought up.

Brandon isn't wasting any more time on Adam today though, he's done his part of the job and now he's a free man. Brandon's going to clean this place up, get a few things set to send to storage, and then move on. There is a beach somewhere far away from here that's calling his name.

First, he cleans the kitchen and boxes up all the food that's left in the cupboards, and all the fridge food he puts in a bag on one of the shelves inside, ready to go when he does. There isn't a ton left over, but it's enough that if Brandon left it all behind, it would go bad and smell something terrible before someone else in his family comes out here to deal with the place. He's got family he plans to mail the keys and a note to once he's settled, but he needs to take care of things for now. He's moved on down the hallway to the living room, and the door is left open and unlocked, when he hears Adam come in and rush down the hall, surprised to see the place left wide open.

Adam can feel his heart beating wildly, and a million thoughts are racing through his head, but he has a feeling the biggest and loudest fear making itself known in there is the one that's true. Demi is gone.

"What's going on? Where's Demi?" He asks anyway, almost yelling, terrified of the answer he's going to get. "Man, I've been trying to call you all morning, why the hell is your cell phone turned off?" Brandon snaps at him in response. "Yes, she's gone home. Her mother called this morning and the kidnapping is done with. Game over. We've got ourselves a shit ton of money, and now we can do whatever the hell we want!"

Adam feels like his heart has been ripped out of his chest at the news, and he slumps down on the couch hard, the wind knocked out of him. He reaches into his pocket and pulls out his cell phone, which has been mostly off since this whole thing started. It just hadn't taken priority for him, and he hasn't even bothered to charge it in days.

"Common man, get your shit together. You look like your cat just died." Brandon says with a laugh, picking up the can of garbage and gathering up some odd scraps to put into it. "I just can't believe I wasn't here, and I didn't know." Adam says, more to himself than anything. "Seriously?" Brandon replies, turning around and setting the trash can on the table for a moment, feeling like his blood's about to boil. He isn't putting up with Adam pining over this girl like a lost love and letting him lose sight of everything else. "You chose not to have your phone on and not to stay in contact, and that's on you my friend. You're the one totally checked out every day until ten whole minutes before I have to leave for work, shutting down and hiding. And that's about as consistent as you get. You're feeling like this because you couldn't handle your hard on around a little hottie and once again, you're a mess because of some girl. What you need to do, is take your million dollars, lay low for a few days, and then get the hell out of here. Take a long vacation somewhere where no one knows your name. And forget all about her."

Adam doesn't say anything to this. He doesn't have to. He takes the scolding because he knows Brandon is right, and then he gets up, helps him with a few things around the house, and then gathers his things and leaves, feeling crappy and rotten with himself. He knows he has no one to blame but himself, and yet, he doesn't feel like he should be responsible at all. He has been drawn to her right from the start in ways that he can't explain, ways that feel totally out of his control. And despite the turmoil that's growing inside of him, he doesn't regret a thing.

Chapter Twenty:
Wednesday Evening

Adam drives around aimlessly for a while, feeling lost without a purpose. Eventually though, his stomach rumbles, and he grabs some take out and heads to his apartment. He has a long hot shower, letting the water go cold around him, too miserable to masturbate but feeling horny none the less, remembering her silky wet hole clenching tightly around his cock. He gets dressed, feeling miserable, and packs two backpacks full of his most must haves, but he doesn't bother to clean out his fridge or worry about the food. He'll figure that out once he has a more secure plan for what he's doing.

He gets on his laptop and logs into his banking system and transfers some of the money around. He'll give Brandon credit for his technology skills; the guy has their banking stuff secured down pat. Yet somehow, the thought of a million dollars in his bank makes Adam feel sad, not happy. This is what he's been working for, but now the whole thing has been tainted by the memory of Demi. He takes his bags, gets in his truck, drives to a nearby ATM and takes some money out, and then he checks himself into a local hotel and crashes on the bed.

The entire ride home in the car, Demi's mother is driving her crazy. She's already ready to jump out and bail on her before they are 3 blocks away from the mall. Her mother cares so much about her reputation, and what people will say if they find out, and how they have to keep this a secret, as if Demi would tell anyone anyway! She just wishes her mother would ask her how she is doing, if she's OK, what she needs now.

Truth be told, Demi doesn't know what she wants or needs now anyway. She gets her mother to stop for takeout at the same burger place that the younger guy had been fond of bringing for them, and she eats while she stares out the window, tuning out her mother as she lectures Demi about processed foods and getting fat.

A short while later, they are home. Back in her childhood home. In her driveway. And staring at her house gives her some awful anxiety. Her mother notices, and finally seems concerned, thinking that her daughters panic attack has something to do with the kidnapping, and being taken at night from her safe place. But in fact, it's something totally different. Demi is remembering all the happy memories that she's had with her father growing up in this house, and how miserable and trapped she's been feeling since his death. She doesn't belong here anymore, and she doesn't even want to go inside right now; the thought of being behind those walls makes her feel more trapped than when she was back at the farm house, kidnapped. But she knows she has to, at least for now, and she breathes deeply, calming herself, and she follows her mother inside.

When she gets to her bedroom, Demi drops the plastic bag she hasn't realized she's still been cradling to her chest. One look around tells her nothing has changed, the bed sheets are still a tossed-up mess from the conflicting dreams she'd been having before they'd grabbed her from sleep, her cell phone is on the end table, and so is the glass of water she had poured herself that night. It all seems like a life time ago.

She leaves her bedroom and grabs a towel, and she hears her mother's voice coming from down the hallway in her office, talking to one of her friends about her vacation. Well, what else would she be talking about right now? Her daughter's kidnapping? That just wouldn't do. Instead of a shower, Demi decides to run herself a hot bubble bath, and she soaks in there until the water goes cold, crying a few times, trying to process everything that's happened and letting everything out of her system.

Afterwards, she dresses in the clothes that she stole from Adam, wondering if he noticed they're missing. Her mother refuses to let her leave the house, so she curls up on the couch and watches TV until her eyes feel like sand paper, not bothering to eat anything for dinner. Her appetite is gone with her spirit; she needs a recharge.

Once it's late enough, she drags herself up the stairs and back into her room, falling into bed. She's exhausted but restless, and she aches for him something terrible. She lets her hand slip down her stomach and under her panties, spreading her lips open, imagining that it's him she's exposed for. She's soaking wet, remembering the thought of him pinning her, taking her, filling her, and she muffles her moans, sliding two of her fingers inside of herself while she rubs her thumb over her clit, driving herself to orgasm, imagining his cock inside of her, his hands, his tongue all over her, taking her again, making her his.

Adam wakes up from his almost coma, consumed by desire for her. He hadn't meant to sleep that long, or that hard, but the last few days have finally caught up with him, and he awakens to darkness outside of the hotel windows. He knows it's stupid, but he grabs his keys, gets in his truck, and drives through the neighborhood towards her house. He knows he isn't going to do anything, not tonight, not with the possibility of anything lingering over them; cops, jail time, detectives, or maybe nothing at all. But just like the feeling of being drawn to her, he can't help himself.

Most of the lights in her house are on, and he drives by a dozen times, thinking about everything that happened this week, from the very first scene in the bedroom, to her foiled escape, to their very, very, hot sex scene on the couch. He wishes so badly that he'd had his phone on this morning, he would have given anything to say goodbye to her. Even if that's all it was, it would have been some kind of closure. As he drives back to the hotel, he's obsessed with the thought that despite all the warnings from Brandon, and all the risks he'll be taking, he has to see her again.

Chapter Twenty-One:
Friday Morning

It only takes two days, and then Demi wakes up on Friday to find her mother busy browsing vacation destinations online at the kitchen table, sipping coffee. Back to ignoring her and continuing on with her regular life. Demi isn't at all surprised to find her mother planning another trip in two weeks. The first night Demi had been home, her mother wouldn't let her leave her sight, even though she didn't want to talk about what happened or actually talk *to* her daughter, by the second day she'd let Demi take the car out to get lunch, and today, it seems like she is back to not caring what happens to her daughter what so ever.

After a quick shower, she gets dressed and throws her hair up in a side braid. She even adds a little make up to her look, just wanting to feel pretty, and different. Then she tells her mother, who's still sitting at the table, now on the phone and her lap top, three cups deep into her pot of coffee, that she's going to the library. Her mother barely gives her a wave, and doesn't look up from what she's doing, so Demi grabs her jacket and her keys and heads out, taking her car and driving around for a little while, trying to decide what she really wants to do. She feels free and lost all at the same time, like she needs to do something, she's capable of doing anything she wants, but she needs to do it *right now*, only she doesn't know what it is.

She drives past the library, but it doesn't call to her. Nothing does. Eventually she finds herself parked at the mall where the older guy had dropped her off. She sits in her car for a while, watching people come and go, the typical hustle and bustle pre-weekend buzz. She thinks about how funny it is that life always goes on, and remembers she felt the same way when her father passed away. School continued. Teachers gave tests. Friends went on dates. Broke up. Holidays came and went. Time never stops, no matter how much you want it to.

She needs to get out of her car before she gets too depressed. She's shed enough tears in the past few days, and now she needs to get her head together and figure out what she's going to do with her life. She feels like this whole ordeal was some kind of second chance for her, and now she needs to move forward.

She wanders over to a coffee shop along the outside of the mall and gets herself a java to go. She sips it slowly, lost in thought, walking along the outskirts of the parking lot, passing the spot where she had met her mother. Demi isn't really paying attention to where she's walking anymore, she just needs to keep her feet moving.

A warm breeze picks up, and she loosens the zipper on her jacket, feeling hot. She imagines what it would be like for it to be her turn to take off on a vacation somewhere, what it would feel like to leave her life for a while, and just lay on the beach, no worries, no cares. She has the money. What adds to her depression is that no one seems to realize that she had sort of did just that, though not on a beach. She had checked out without telling anyone for almost an entire week. Other than a few hey how have you been messages on her phone, no one was at all concerned that she'd done so, even if it wasn't willingly. She doubts anyone is going to care too much if she does it again, this time by her own choosing.

She crosses the parking lot where she was dropped off by Brandon, but she's no longer thinking about the kidnapping, now she's lost in thoughts about a hot beach, and she decides when she goes home she's going to plug in her tablet and start researching her own beach vacations. The thought makes her smile, it's the first true happy thought she's had in a few days. It gives her a sense of control and purpose with her life again. But as she passes the bike racks and the path that leads into the forest, that happy thought is snatched from her as strong hands grab her roughly and pull her into the forest, and then a gloved hand covers her mouth, so she can't scream.

A million thoughts run through her head, but mostly it's, "Seriously, again?!" She's in complete disbelief that something like this could happen to her a second time. And then she's spun around and looking directly into his eyes, the younger one's eyes, the same deep blue eyes she's been thinking about and yet forcing herself not to think about for days. The hand that's pinning her tightly and the hand that's covering her mouth are the same hands that she can't stop thinking about having all over her, and how they made her feel. Suddenly she goes weak, like her knees may give out on her.

Adam takes a quick look around, making sure no one has seen them, and then he lets her go and takes a little step away from her, giving her some space. He doesn't know if she'll be happy to see him, or if she'll want to slap him, or run away screaming for the police. But he's here, and he's ready to take his chances.

Demi looks him up and down, taking him in, her heart beating fast, breathing heavy, and still feeling a little bit scared. But as much as she is beside herself with happiness to see him, to have him here, she can't help bursting out in laughter, hard, holding her stomach and doubling over. Adam is so confused by her laughter, and finds himself looking around them, trying to see what he's missed, what she could possibly find so funny at a time like this. It doesn't look like she's going to stop laughing any time soon, every time she opens her mouth to talk, she just starts laughing again, and he can't take it anymore. "Demi, what are you laughing at?" he asks, nervously.

"You," she says, gasping for air and wiping her tears, and when he looks offended, almost hurt, she calms down and is quick to continue. "I mean, look at you! Look at all this trouble that you've gone to! Did you follow me here??" He glances down at her gesture and sees his outfit from her eyes; a black hoodie, black hat pulled down low under the hood, black jeans, black shoes, black gloves. Now that he thinks about it, he looks like he's on his way to a bank robbery. "I just wanted to keep a low profile, I guess I went a little too far," he says in his own defense. "And yes, I followed you here, I had to talk to you, I needed to see you, and I thought it would be safest alone."

"There's no need though," she replies, "My mother kept her word and never went to the police, or anyone, so there's no one to hide from. She's far too scared to ruin her own reputation, she would *never* want wind of what happened to get out. Nope, she babied me for about five whole minutes, and now she's planning her next trip to Mexico, or the Dominican, or wherever the hell she feels like going to this time."

Adam can't believe how thrilled he is to hear this and feels a ton of stress wash away that he wasn't even aware he was carrying. He and Brandon are actually going to get away with this. They are going to get away with a two-million-dollar kidnapping. And maybe there's a chance he can still have the girl, too. What would it matter to Brandon now, if no one ever knows, and he's halfway to the beach somewhere anyway?

A few moments of silence pass as tension builds between them, both of them just looking at each other, listening to the faint sound of traffic in the distance and the birds in the forest. They are both burning with a thousand questions to ask, but neither of them knows what to say first.

Finally, she breaks it, asking something that's really bugging her; Why did he come back? Why is he here? Here she has been killing herself over not asking the older guy what their names were, if she could or should contact him, what was going to happen, if maybe the younger one liked her. She had spent the last two days trying to forget what had happened, trying to get him out of her mind, and yet every night she still sleeps in his clothes, and drives herself crazy with unanswered questions and regret.

And now here he is again, right in front of her, and she's damned if she is going to let anything go unanswered again if she can help it.

"I, I honestly don't really know, other than I just had to see you again." He stammers, feeling nervous and put on the spot, but determined to tell her anything, everything, whatever it takes. "I have so many questions, and so many things I don't know, and don't understand, and I just needed to talk to you again, I *had* to see you again. I couldn't just leave, it was driving me crazy." He stops himself from rambling, feeling his face grow red, and finds that she's staring at him intently. "I have another question," she asks. "Anything," he answers, taking a step closer to her. "What's your name?"

The question takes him by surprise, and then he realizes that she still wouldn't know. What an odd thing, he thinks, to have gone through all of this and not even know the person's name? "Adam," he replies. She's still looking at him, saying the name in her head, trying it on him for size, and then she opens her mouth and says his name back to him, softly, "Adam."

The way it comes out tightens his stomach in knots, releasing butterflies, and gives him a half chub, realizing how much he loves to hear her say it, and how much he'd love to hear her moan it. Swallowing hard, he leans in and kisses her, cupping her by the back of the neck and pulling her close, pushing his tongue deep into her mouth, pressing them up against the tree, eager to be with her again.

To Be Continued…

I hope you've enjoyed this novel. If you're anxious for more, don't forget to check out the sequel, HEIST.

Please follow me on social media, Lady Mack Xo, and don't forget to head on over to my website for news, free stories, blogs and more!

www.ladymackxo.com

Thanks again!

Much Love,
Author Carissa McIntyre,
Lady Mack Xo